Whispers of Healing

BOOK FOUR IN THE WHISPERS OF NEW ENGLAND SERIES

SUE MILLS

Choose The Front Row Media

Blurbs

"Sam Carpenter's day-to-day as a newly minted co-parent to his young daughter will resonate with anyone whose family life hasn't always lived up to their ideals. Whether addressing the emotional toll of healing childhood traumas or the deep desire to experience love while doing right by a child, Sam's journey in *Whispers of Healing* is unique to him yet universal in its imperfections." Libybet R. G., Proofreader, Red Adept Editing

To my brothers, Kevin, Steven and Jason Meilleur
We've had brief periods of estrangement (nothing like Sam's)
and our mother's biggest fear was that we'd have nothing to do
with each other
when she and my father were gone. Thankfully that's not the
case and I count them
as some of the most important people in my life.

Author's Note

Thank you for picking up Whispers of Healing.

This is the fourth book in the Whispers of New England series and together with the fifth book, Whispers of Change, coming in May, form a duet that tells Sam's story.

Healing begins where Whispers of Forgiveness ends, with Sam returning to an empty house. It runs parallel to books two and three, Mistletoe and Starlight and will share some scenes with those books but will dive into Sam's point of view.

These books came about because I love Sam, and when Quinn ended up with Caden, I couldn't leave Sam's story untold. I hope you enjoy reading this as much as I enjoyed writing it.

Playlist

Stick Season – Noah Kahan

Memories – Maroon 5

Maroon – Taylor Swift

Die With a Smile – Lady Gaga, Bruno Mars

Northern Attitude – Noah Kahan

Dial Drunk – Noah Kahan, Post Malone

Story of My Life – One Direction

Beautiful Things – Benson Boone

Photograph – Ed Sheeran

She Calls Me Back – Noah Kahan

Contents

Chapter One

The Note

SAM CARPENTER TURNED ONTO the winding dirt road, his good mood from that afternoon ebbing. Not even the surprise reunion with Quinn Michaels, his first love, was enough to ward off the despondence that had been nipping at him since he left Boston. The drive home to Vermont had been long, and as Sam pulled up to his very dark house, despair engulfed him.

It was not supposed to be like this. His daughter, Piper, should be opening the door and jumping into his arms, shouting about how much she missed him. In his fantasy world, all traces of her stutter would be gone. When he'd planned the trip to the Healthy Living in the Workplace conference in Boston, Sam hoped that the time apart would ease the tension between him and Piper's mother, Norah, his partner of eight years. That theory didn't even get to be tested. Instead, five days earlier, as he walked out the door, Norah had told him she and Piper wouldn't be there when he returned.

Sam climbed out of the car slowly, digging for the house key in his pocket. He hesitated to open the door—walking into that empty house would make it all real. Norah had called the day before and told him she had moved out everything that she'd brought into their home, including Piper's bed.

Finally, his shaking hand worked the lock, and the door swung open. On autopilot, he flipped a switch, and light flooded the mudroom. "At least she didn't take the light bulbs," he muttered, dropping his duffel and backpack to the floor.

After wandering into the kitchen, Sam noticed a colorful stone he'd found on the first hike he and Norah had taken, over eight years ago, sitting on the counter. "What the... She kept that on her desk."

When he walked closer, he saw the rock was anchoring a note.

S

The house I've rented is at 106 Rock Maple Road.

I hate that we've come to this, but the tension between us has become intolerable, and I can't watch our precious little girl sink any lower because of our actions. I know, in the depths of your heart, you feel the same way.

My lease is for six months. Maybe that will be long enough...

I'll always love you.

N

Sam propped his elbow on the counter and lowered his forehead to his fist, gripping the note in his other hand. After a few moments, he straightened, crumpled the paper into a ball, and opened the cupboard where they kept a wastebasket, only to find it empty. He shook his head. "Of course. Everything is gone." He tossed the scrunched-up note into a corner of the kitchen.

Sam made his way through the house, opening the kitchen cabinets to find only a few plates and bowls, a couple of pots and pans, a coffee mug, and two glasses. The dining room was empty, but the living room still had the couch, recliner, and television—all things Sam had purchased. Both his bedroom and Piper's were completely devoid of furniture.

A trip back to the car yielded bedding purchased on his way home as well as a six-pack of beer, a takeout pizza, and a sack of groceries. The bedding joined his bags on the floor. Sam took the pizza and a can of beer into the living room and sank down onto the couch, where he popped the top on the beer and took a long swallow.

Looking around, Sam rubbed his hand over his jaw. *Damn.* He shook his head. *I'm thirty-one years old and have nothing to show for it.* He took another sip of his beer. *Except for Piper.* He would always have her.

His bite of pizza caught in his throat, and he shoved the rest of the slice back into the box. He chugged the beer, and in a sudden fit of despair, he threw the can across the room. As it bounced off the opposite wall, echoing in the hollowness of the room, Sam rested his elbows on his knees and dropped his head into his hands, emotionally exhausted.

Taking a deep breath, he slumped back on the couch, looking across to where the can had landed—under his drafting table. His degree from Winthrop University, which Norah had insisted he frame, still hung on the wall, along with the sketch from his final design project. *I worked my ass off in that architecture program. She can't take that away from me.*

After a few minutes, Sam rose and walked to the kitchen with a heavy tread. He stood at the island, staring at the ball of paper in the corner, mocking him. Taking a deep breath, he picked it up and smoothed it out on the counter. *106 Rock Maple. She isn't far from here.* He drank another beer while standing at the counter, trying to figure out a path forward.

Another can called his name, and he reached for it then pulled back. *Pip's going to be here in the morning. I need to be ready.*

Sam's fingers ran over the words on the paper as if trying to feel them. He picked up the rock that Norah had placed on top of the note and pictured her. She'd started to write then paused, raising the pen to her face and tapping it on her chin as she thought about the words she would use. He'd seen her do that hundreds of times.

Then, before she walked out the door for the final time, she took the stone, *their* stone, and placed it on top of the paper.

Damn it, Norah! How do you do this to me? I thought I had clarity, and now I'm tied up in knots—again. He picked up the note and shoved it in a drawer.

Returning to the couch, Sam fired off several quick texts before pulling a blanket up to his chin and falling asleep.

> Hope you got home okay.

> Bought those inflatable mattresses we talked about.

> I miss you.

> I was hoping to hear from you tonight.

> Talk tomorrow?

Sam awoke the next morning to a text from Quinn.

> I'm home and heading to bed. Catch up tomorrow.

His heart warmed. *I must have fallen asleep as soon as I sent that last text.* While he readied the house for Piper's arrival, he sent more texts.

At nine, the front door opened, and Piper ran in shouting, "D-D-Daddy! D-Daddy-O, where are you?"

Sam came out of his bedroom, lifted her over his head, then brought her down into a tight hug. "There's my girl. I missed you so much!" Piper squirmed, and he released her.

"I m-missed you too, Daddy." She looked at her mother, who'd followed her inside. "C-can I have breakfast now?"

Norah pulled a box of cereal and a milk carton out of the tote bag she was carrying. "Piper didn't want to eat at home because she was eager to see you. I knew you wouldn't have anything." She went to the cabinet for a bowl then saw the box of Shredded Wheat on the counter and turned toward Sam. "What..."

"I shopped on my way home." He struggled to keep his tone light. "I figured you hadn't left any food." Sam lifted Piper onto a stool at the island.

"Am I going to sleep on the floor, Daddy?" Piper asked.

"Of course not. Would I let my best girl sleep on the floor? I bought a cool mattress for you to sleep on with *Paw Patrol* sheets. It's all ready for you." When he looked at Norah, he recognized the look in her eyes. Sam sneered. "Do you want to make sure it's okay?"

Norah started to speak, looked toward Piper's bedroom, and stopped without saying anything.

"My God, you don't trust me to make a bed for my daughter?" he asked, keeping his voice low so Piper couldn't hear. "You are unbelievable!" He shook his head in disgust then turned away and spoke more loudly. "Hey, Pip, come on! Let's go check out your bedroom."

When Piper saw the inflatable mattress, she squealed and threw herself down on it. "C-c-can I jump on it?"

"I'm afraid not, peanut," Sam said. "This is for sleeping, not jumping." He looked at Norah and muttered, "Does it meet with your approval?"

"It's fine," Norah hissed. "Don't forget that bedtime is seven thirty. And we should talk about visitation."

Sam glared at her, fire burning in his stomach, before turning to his daughter. "Piper, I think it's time for *Peppa Pig*. Come to the living room to watch while Mommy and Daddy go outside for a minute."

After Piper settled on the couch, he motioned for Norah to join him outside. "Do you consider it visitation when Piper is with you?" His voice was calm, and he hoped it hid his anger.

Norah shook her head. "No, of course not."

"Then it damn well is not 'visitation' when she's with me! I'm her father, and I want her with me half the time." Sam rubbed his hand against his jaw. "I don't need to be reminded about bedtime. You're acting like I haven't been a part of her life from the beginning—the *beginning*, Norah! I'm not about to step away now just because you moved out."

"You're angry."

Sam looked away. He felt like she was mocking him with her icy tone dripping with sarcasm. The same tone she used in every argument. "Hell yes, I'm angry! You blindsided me Monday morning."

"We talked about separating when we were in counseling. We both agreed it would be the best thing for all of us."

"Yes, but we've had zero conversations about what that was going to look like. When I moved to Jerry's cabin in the summer, we discussed every facet. Where I was going, how Piper would split her time, how we would stay in touch. Every. Bit." His clenched fist pounded into the open palm of his other hand twice to emphasize each word. "This time, you rented a place and arranged for the move to happen *while I was gone* and presented it to me as a *fait accompli*."

"I told you I wasn't going to wait any longer. One of us needed to make a move, and I realized it wasn't going to be you."

"I can't believe you did this." Sam looked into her brown eyes. Once, they'd held warmth for him—now he saw nothing there. "I don't want to spend any more time on this right now. I want Piper on Monday and Tuesday nights and every other weekend. On Wednesday nights, I'm going to Jesse's, and

Thursday can be a late night at work, so the beginning of the week works best for me."

"That means I'll go from Friday to Wednesday without seeing her every other week. That's five nights!"

Finally, a little emotion erupted from her. "And I'll go five nights without seeing her when you have her on the weekend. You started this, Norah. It's a fair split."

"Fine, for now. Have you contacted a lawyer?"

"I got here late last night. It's on my list for next week."

"Since when do you make lists?" When Sam didn't answer, she sighed. "We'll need to go to a mediator, and they will sort out visita—the time split."

"Whatever. I'm done with this for today. I haven't seen my daughter in a week, and I want to spend time with her. Did you bring her clothes?" He strode to Norah's car to retrieve Piper's bag.

Norah returned inside to kiss her goodbye and left after saying she would call in the evening.

Sam carried the bag to Piper's room and sat on the mattress, trying to get his emotions under control. He looked around the room. *This is pitiful, but I'm going to make it work.* His eyes landed on the one picture Norah hadn't removed. The three of them were standing on a dock, smiling happily at the camera. A friend had taken it during the summer when he had faith things would work out between him and Norah. *What a joke.*

He joined Piper on the couch. Running one hand down her long brown hair, he smiled at the precocious six-year-old, who had his own light-blue eyes.

She climbed onto his lap, and he calmed down further while they watched television together.

After a moment, she looked up at him. "D-Daddy, why did we have to m-move? I don't like it. All my stuff is in boxes, and I can't find my stuffed animals." Her stutter had developed a year and a half earlier, and no amount of speech therapy seemed to help.

Sam's heart broke a little more. "Mommy and I need to find a way to be nicer to each other. It's like when I went to the cabin during the summer. Remember how much fun we had when I was living there?"

"But this isn't like that. You d-didn't take all the furniture, and I knew where my stuff was."

"Well, the cabin had furniture, so I didn't need to take anything. You needed to bring the furniture with you so you aren't living in an empty house."

"But we left *you* an empty house."

"Yes, and that let me buy those cool mattresses for us to sleep on. I'll be fine. But we need to buy more groceries. I'm going to make a list, then we'll go out for burgers before we go shopping. You can watch one more show."

Sam walked to the kitchen. The confrontation with Norah reinforced the realization he'd reached in Boston. Their relationship was over. They weren't good for each other. The anger she stirred in him reminded him of his father, the last person on earth Sam wanted to emulate. And her icy demeanor was nothing like that of the woman he'd fallen in love with eight years earlier.

He thought about Norah's sarcastic jab after she asked him about a lawyer. *Since when do I make lists? Since I ran into Quinn at the conference and she helped me see what life could look like without you.* While making a grocery list, Sam thought about the week in Boston.

He had arrived at the first conference session late, frazzled, and still reeling from Norah's announcement. He'd found an open seat in the back row of the darkened lecture hall, struggling to control his emotions. When the lights came up, Sam discovered he was sitting next to Quinn Michaels, his first love. Ten years earlier, they'd each broken the other's heart in a wrenching breakup, but Sam had never forgotten Quinn, and Norah knew it. She had always accused him of having unfinished business with Quinn, and as much as Sam denied it, he'd known she was right.

Sam had invited Quinn to dinner the first night to catch up, and over the course of the week, they'd healed old hurts and discovered they lived only twenty miles apart. On their last night, they ended up in bed, joining their bodies as they had when they were together and in ways they had never thought of back then. The next day, they took advantage of Quinn's late checkout time from the hotel to go at each other again. Besotted with the physical connection they felt, they agreed to see each other after their return from Boston.

Sam finished the grocery list, shaking his head. *While Norah was writing me a note, I was with the one person in the world she's jealous of.* He wasn't proud of having jumped into bed with Quinn, but their reconnection had eased an ache that had been burning in him for years.

Chapter Two

An Invitation

S AM DROVE THE TWENTY miles from his house in eastern Vermont into Hanover, New Hampshire, then continued to West Lebanon, where there was a large grocery store and several strip malls. As they crossed the Connecticut River, which formed the border between the two states, Piper said excitedly, "Look, D-D-Daddy, the rowers are still out there."

His heart warmed thinking about the times during the summer when they had sat in a riverside park, watching the sleek sculls make their way up and down the waterway.

At the Walmart Supercenter, the two of them wandered the aisles, buying enough food to fill his cabinets and the fridge. Sam secretly hoped they would run into Quinn. *Pip shouldn't meet her yet, but oh, what I would give to talk to her for a couple of minutes.*

"D-D-Daddy." Piper's voice pulled him out of his thoughts. "C-c-can we buy a game?" She was holding two board games Sam remembered had been in her room before Norah moved out. When he nodded, she placed them in the cart.

Sam added a few books he knew she liked then picked up a teddy bear. "Hey, Piper Carpenter," he growled, pretending to be the bear. "Can I come home with you? Pretty please?"

"Silly D-Daddy." She laughed and grabbed the bear out of his hands, hugging it tightly.

They entered a sporting-goods store, where Sam asked the clerk to measure Piper for skis and boots. Quinn had mentioned skiing back in Boston, and it had stirred something in Sam. He wanted to ski this winter and planned to teach Piper.

Back at home, Sam found a televised ski race. He pointed to the screen. "I used to ski like that."

"That fast?"

They were watching an Olympic qualifying race for the giant slalom event, and the skiers were flying down the slope.

"Definitely not that fast, but I was good at it. I'm going to try it again this winter. See if I still remember how. Would you like to go with me? We'd go to the mountain near where I grew up."

A skier missed one of the gates and careened into the fencing that outlined the course.

Piper cringed. "It l-looks scary."

"You wouldn't be on hills that steep to start. It's a little scary, but it's lots of fun too."

"You'd be with m-me?"

"Of course."

Sam thought about how his life had become consumed with work and home. *There's no reason that family time can't include something like this. It did for us before Dad sank into the bottle.* Sam and his brothers learned how to ski from their parents, and the five of them had spent many happy weekends on the mountain when Sam was in elementary school.

"What about M-M-Mommy?" Piper asked.

"She was never interested in it." Sam ruffled Piper's hair. "This would be something for you and me."

"Okay. I love you, D-Daddy." She pulled away from him. "C-can I go play?"

The phone rang Sunday morning as Piper shouted, "Go fish!" at the beginning of their fifth round of the card game. Sam took a deep breath when he saw *Mom* on his caller ID.

He tried to remember the last time he had seen his mother, Laura. It was at Aunt Michelle's house, celebrating Grandad's birthday, and he'd gone alone. *God, that was way back in February. She never gives up on me, no matter how long it's been.*

Sam's estrangement from his family started when he was in high school and had worsened in tandem with his father's alcohol abuse. By the time Piper was born, Sam had stopped pretending he had a relationship with his father. Sadly, his once-close bond with his two brothers had also fallen victim to the rift.

Sam grew up an hour north of his current home, in an area known as the Northeast Kingdom. Tucked into the northeastern corner of the state, bumping up against the Canadian and New Hampshire borders, the area was remote, riddled with poverty, and sparsely populated. His mother and father still lived in his boyhood home, but Sam hadn't been there in years.

"Hi, Mom," he said into the phone as Piper slid off the couch to the floor and began playing with her toy barn and farm animals.

"Hi, Sam." His mother's voice was always warm. "Wondered how you are. It's been a while."

"I'm fine. Busy. You know how it is."

"Uh-huh. How's my granddaughter? I'd love to see her. She must be so much bigger than the last time we saw her."

Sam noticed how his mother hadn't said, *we'd like to see her.* "Piper's amazing. Taking first grade by storm, going to gymnastics lessons—and she just finished the youth soccer season." Pride oozed from his voice. "She's crazy about animals. Right now, she's playing with a barn and pretending to make all the animal sounds."

"I'd love a picture," Laura said, her voice wistful. "I'm calling to invite you for Thanksgiving. Matt and Jilly will be here. And Joe too."

"I don't know, Mom." His stomach clenched the way it always did when he thought about his family.

She sighed. "Joe's been here often this year. He and your father have a project they are working on. They'd like to show it to you."

"Yeah, Joe texted me a few times about coming up."

Sam considered the invitation. *I have nothing else to do. Norah's taking Piper to Connecticut, and Quinn already told me Thanksgiving is a workday for her. I don't want to be alone. I guess if Joe's been dealing with Dad all year, I can put up with the old man for a couple of hours.*

"Yeah, I'll come, but it'll just be me," he said. "Norah and Piper are going to Connecticut to spend the holiday with her family."

"I'm so glad," she said. Sam could hear the happiness in her voice, a stark contrast to what he was feeling. They chatted briefly about his trip to Boston before he ended the call, saying, "Bye, Mom. I'll see you on Thanksgiving, probably late morning."

"It'll be nice to have you here, Sam. I love you."

He thought about how his mother never ended a call without saying, "I love you," as he joined Piper on the floor.

Half an hour later, his phone rang again, and he smirked at the caller ID. *Carpenter's Carpentry.* Years ago, his brother Joe had labeled his number that way when he started working as a finish carpenter for a large construction firm near Boston. "Hey, Joe."

"Hey, little brother." Joe was one year older than Sam and never let him forget it. "What's up with you coming to the city and not getting in touch?"

"I didn't have any free time. The entire week was tightly scheduled." That wasn't altogether true. He'd found time to see Quinn every night. "You're going to Mom and Dad's for Turkey Day?"

"Yeah, and I hear you're coming by yourself. How long is Norah in Connecticut?"

"She's going to be there until Sunday."

"Why don't you stay up north for the weekend, come to camp with me?" Joe asked.

"Camp? I haven't hunted since I was in high school!" The family hunting camp was a run-down cabin that was over fifty years old. All three boys had grown up going there to hunt white-tailed deer every fall.

"I'm not going to hunt. I've spent quite a bit of time there this year. Dad and I have been making some improvements. I need to finish some things, and I could use your help. Plus, I'd like you to see what we've done."

"You're looking for free labor, huh? Is Dad going to be there?" Sam wasn't interested in spending a weekend trapped with his father in the small cabin.

"No, he's going to Uncle John's camp after dinner and hunting all weekend."

"I guess I can. I have nothing else to do." Then Sam remembered that several months earlier, his mother had let it slip that Joe and his wife had separated. "How are you, anyway? First Thanksgiving without the wife. Must suck."

"I'm okay. It was rough at first, but we've been resolving the financial details. We put the house on the market in October and had an offer in two weeks. It'll close in the middle of December. I moved into an apartment a couple of months ago, and Tina has taken a job in Atlanta. She'll move her stuff after Thanksgiving, so we have little left to do. The divorce will be finalized in January. Thank God no kids are involved."

Sam motioned to Piper that he would be right back as he walked toward his bedroom. "Well, to tell you my complete story, Norah moved out while I was in Boston. She took almost everything in the house. We need to work out all the details, like how we'll share Piper and disentangle our finances."

"Sorry to hear that. Was this sudden? I thought you were solid."

"No, we've been way less than solid for a few years. I moved out for a couple of months in the summer. Things seemed better, so I moved back." He sighed. "Now we're right back to where we were. I'm not ready to tell Mom and Dad, so can you keep it quiet?"

"Of course," Joe said. "It's not my story to tell. I'll see you on Thanksgiving, and we'll do some hammer therapy at camp. I've found pounding nails works out a lot of anger."

"Hammer therapy." Sam chuckled. "I like that. I need it. See you then."

Chapter Three

Quinn's First Visit

LATE WEDNESDAY AFTERNOON, SAM jumped out of his car and rushed into the house while he checked his phone for the time. *Thank God. I've got fifteen minutes before Quinn is supposed to arrive.* He opened the refrigerator and took out the vegetables he'd been working on when he was called away. After doing the finishing touches, he added them to the chicken already in the oven.

Frazzled, Sam looked around, just as he had in the morning, trying to figure out if the house looked suitable enough for company. One of the constant problems between him and Norah was his messiness. There was so little in the house now that it wasn't difficult to see the things that needed to be put away. He took a deep breath. *It's not company—it's Quinn.* Relief that he'd managed to get back before Quinn arrived flooded over him again. *How embarrassing it would have been if she had gotten here before me.*

He had texted Jesse on Monday to let him know dinner on Wednesday was out. Jesse was his best friend and the only person Sam had talked to about the disintegration of his relationship with Norah. Jesse knew Sam would have a hard time adjusting to being alone and invited him to come for dinner once a week. He appreciated Jesse and his wife's generous offer, but when Norah had Piper, Sam planned to be with Quinn. He was confident talking things out with Jesse wouldn't be necessary now that Quinn was in his life.

Sam and Quinn had exchanged text messages during the week, with him sending many more than he received. She had suggested that they go out for dinner, but he wanted her here, at his house, so they could have private time. He would cook for her.

Sam opened the garage door as Quinn entered the driveway, and he walked out to her car. She rolled down her window, and Sam leaned in. "You can park in the garage."

"I don't need to do that. I can only stay for a couple of hours."

"Please?" He leaned in farther and lightly kissed her lips.

She teased, "Is your HOA going to get after you for having a car in the driveway?"

Sam grinned. "No, but nosy neighbors might. I've already had a couple of questions about where Norah is. If you don't mind, I'd rather not have to explain anything else. At least, not right away."

"That makes sense." They had joked about local rumor mills and gossip while they were in Boston. She waved her hand, signaling for him to move away from the car. He followed her into the garage, closed the door, and led her into the house. He put his arms around her, and she melted against him.

Quinn murmured. "I've been looking forward to this all week." He backed away and gently unzipped her jacket. She shrugged it off, and Sam hung it on a hook in the mudroom. His arms went around her again, and his lips sought hers. The kiss was tentative, the same way his first one had been the week before.

Sam shifted slightly and said, "This is all I've thought about since Friday." He took her hand to lead her from the mudroom to the kitchen. He extended his other arm with a flourish and said, "Welcome to Casa Carpenter."

Quinn looked around, and Sam knew she was trying to take it all in and comparing it to the pictures he had shown her the week before. "This is really nice. The photos don't do it justice. Show me the rest."

A smile blossomed across his face as they walked toward the living room, where a stone fireplace dominated the space. "It looked different when it had more furniture and pictures on the walls."

Quinn took his hand. "Strangely, I like seeing it this way. You can see the bones of the space. Did you do the fireplace? And why no fire? I have a fire almost every night."

"Yes, I did the fireplace. It took a solid month, every night after work and every weekend." He ran his hand over the stones. "I had to run out for a bit earlier. Got back just before you arrived. That's why there's no fire. I..."

"You what?"

He shook his head. "Never mind. It's not important." He turned to walk toward the bedrooms, but Quinn stopped him.

"Is that a drafting table?" She walked over to the corner. On the top were several drawings of a commercial property. "Did you do these?"

Sam had a degree in architecture and worked as a project manager for an economic development company. "I did some of them. It's our latest project, and I'm trying to pull it all together."

"I always loved it when you came home from college and showed me the sketches you'd done during the week." Sam had been in college and Quinn in high school for most of the time they dated.

He chuckled. "I eventually heard that inviting a woman up to your room to see your etchings was a sexual come-on back in the fifties or sixties. I was horrified because I felt like asking you to look at my sketches was the same thing. And that wasn't my intention!"

Quinn laughed, saying, "I heard that and had the same thought." Their eyes met, and leaning forward, he brought his lips to hers. This kiss was much less tentative than the one they'd shared earlier.

Sam ran his hands up and down her back and then, with his arm around her waist, led her down the hall to the bedrooms. "This is Pip's room." He pointed at the teddy bear sitting on top of the mattress. "She was upset on Saturday because all her stuff was in boxes at the new place, so when we went shopping, I bought that bear." Quinn snuggled closer against him as they walked to his room.

They sat on the inflatable mattress and came together again. Sam's tongue was insistent, and after a few seconds, Quinn's lips parted, inviting him in. He played and explored for several minutes. His hand slid under her sweater to stroke her back. "Your skin is so soft." He nuzzled her neck as his hand moved to her front, pushing her sweater up so his fingers could move under her bra. He pinched her nipple and felt it pebble in response, but the rest of her body felt frozen.

Sam lifted his head to look into Quinn's eyes. "What's wrong?" She cocked her head, silently questioning him. "Your nipple responded, but the rest of you didn't. You're holding back."

She sighed. "I was enjoying talking to you, seeing your house, but now I feel like this is the only thing you wanted to see me for." Trying to lighten the mood, she said, "And I thought you were going to feed me. Whatever you're cooking smells delicious."

Sam dragged her sweater down and stood up, placing her feet on the floor. "Let's go check on that chicken." Quinn followed him to the kitchen and stood at the island while Sam opened the oven door and removed a pan holding a golden-brown chicken, potatoes, and vegetables. He put it on top of the stove, laid a sheet of foil over it, and walked to the island. "That needs to sit for a few minutes."

He leaned on his elbows. "Quinn, I want to have sex with you, but I want so much more. I never want you to think sex is all I want. If it's not what you want, then we won't. But I thought you were as into it as I was in Boston."

"I was." She drummed her fingers on the counter. "I don't know. Something about you rejecting my invitation to go out to dinner and then coming on so strongly in your bedroom rubbed me the wrong way. And I realized you were with Norah here less than two weeks ago."

Sam sighed. "Yeah, I was. But not happily. And there's not a trace of her left here. She took everything. I want to spend time with you, but not at a noisy restaurant. What can I do to make you more comfortable? We'll go as fast or slow as you want."

"I appreciate that. How did it go when you saw her?"

"Saturday was rough. She was icy cold, and it made me angry that she wants to work out a visitation schedule. Visitation! I don't consider it a visitation when I'm with Pip. I'm her dad!"

Quinn reached out to stroke his cheek, and her compassion filled his heart. Sam took Quinn's hand. "You said you can only stay a couple of hours. I don't want to spend it talking about Norah. Tell me about how it was being back at the hospital after being away for a week. I came back to a desk full of paperwork."

While Quinn told him about the hospital, Sam sliced the chicken and brought out plates and silverware. They ate at the island, and in response to Quinn's question about his cooking skills, Sam explained Norah had insisted on a split of household duties and cooking had been his responsibility.

After Quinn helped him put the leftovers away, he put his arms around her. "How late can you stay?"

"Another half hour or so." She nuzzled his neck.

Still hugging her, he shuffled them over to the cupboard. He opened it and pulled out a wine glass. "I bought this with you in mind. Norah literally left me two glasses, two plates, and so on. Just enough for Piper and me." Quinn put her hand on his cheek. He appreciated her attempt to soften his anger. "I know you like wine, and I wouldn't make you drink it out of a plastic cup. Let's sit in the living room." He opened the fridge, poured wine into the glass, and opened a beer for himself.

They sat on the couch. "Come here—I'll behave this time," he said, pulling her into his lap. They brought their lips together and spent several minutes exploring. He rubbed her back but did not go any further. "I wish you were staying overnight. I enjoyed sharing the bed with you in Boston."

"My shift starts at six a.m., and you live twenty miles away. It would make my morning too complicated." She returned to kissing his lips.

"What about the weekend? Will you stay then?"

"I absolutely need to work on my research paper this weekend."

"I have some work I'll be bringing home. We can both do what we need to."

"Why don't you come to my townhouse? I have a bed." Her tone was humorous.

"You don't like my minimalist look?"

"Oh no, it's all the style. But seriously, have you decided what you're going to do as far as furniture or if you are going to stay here?"

"No, there's so much to figure out it overwhelms me. So, I think about you instead." He grinned at her. "Back to the weekend. Being here works better for me because my drafting table is here. I'll be working on some projects that I need to do plans and sketches for."

"I have a cat. He misses me if I'm gone."

"Seriously, a cat? That will keep you from staying with me?"

"He's still recovering from me being away last week." She rolled her shoulders and looked around. "I have a table in my dining room. You'd have plenty of room to work. I was teasing before about having a bed, but seriously, won't we be more comfortable on a bed?"

Sam rubbed his jaw. "Those twenty miles that are keeping you from staying? They're a problem for me too."

"How so?"

"Pip's having a hard time adjusting. I had to have Norah come over Monday night because Pip couldn't stop crying. And the same thing happened late this afternoon at Norah's. I'd been over there just before you arrived. That's why I didn't have time to start a fire." He gazed into Quinn's eyes. "The place Norah rented is only three miles from here. I don't feel like I can be twenty miles away. I'm sorry because I'd love to see your place. And sleep in a proper bed." He smiled at her.

Sam watched Quinn's eyes cloud over. "I shouldn't come over, then. I don't want to put you in a bad spot."

"No, don't say that. I want to spend time with you. Remember saying we were insulated at the conference?" She nodded. "I agreed with you, and this is life intruding. But we can handle it. Calming her down doesn't take long. Monday night, she just wanted a kiss goodnight from her mommy. It hasn't been every night. I don't want to miss the chance of an entire weekend with you."

There was a pause before Quinn answered. "We knew this would be complicated. Did you go through this last summer?"

Sam rubbed the back of his neck. "No. I think that seemed temporary. I was just away at camp. Her life wasn't totally disrupted."

Quinn relented. "I can come over. Max will be okay for a couple of days. I'll bring takeout. Do you like Thai food?"

He nodded and then added, "How about tomorrow night? Can you come over?"

"I have dinner plans with a friend. We go out every other week."

"Please." He tried to keep the pleading tone out of his voice but knew he failed. "I want to be with you as much as possible."

"One of my personal tenets is not to change plans because a better offer comes along, so no."

"Ah, but you admit I'm a better offer."

She smiled and shrugged her shoulders before looking away from him. "Do you remember Caden Brady from Harvard?"

"The doctor we had lunch with? Yeah, what about him?" Dr. Brady had been charming, and Sam remembered how captivated Quinn had been by him.

"He invited me out to dinner that night. I turned him down because I already had plans with you."

"That was the night you took me to bed. So, which one of us was the better offer?"

"I guess I'll never know." She struggled to stand up, but his arms kept her in his lap. "I have to head home so I can get some sleep." He reluctantly stood up and hugged her tightly before letting her go.

Sam watched her back out of the garage, and she rolled down her window. "Just a reminder. My phone is in my locker all day. I don't see any of your messages."

Well, that didn't go as I planned. He had expected more of the wild sex they had in Boston. Just thinking about their last afternoon made him hard. But as she reminded him, they needed to get to know each other again.

Chapter Four

Plans Interrupted

SAM PACED, EAGER FOR Quinn to arrive. She was already half an hour later than she had been on Wednesday. He had reduced the number of texts he sent, which was difficult when she occupied his every waking thought. He was cautiously optimistic that Piper was adjusting, since he hadn't had to go to Norah's house on Thursday.

When Quinn finally arrived, Sam opened her car door and, after a quick hug, picked up the takeout bags. Inside, he placed them on the island and turned to Quinn, opening his arms. "Come here. I need a proper hug." He wrapped his arms around her and nuzzled her neck.

Quinn melted against him, and he savored her warmth. Her hands ran up and down his back. When they parted, she said, "I wasn't sure what you'd like, so I bought a variety. We'll probably have enough for lunch tomorrow."

"It smells great. How was your dinner last night?"

Quinn smiled. "It was yummy. We went to the restaurant you refused to go to on Wednesday night. Maybe you and I can go there sometime."

Sam didn't answer, and Quinn asked, "Did you bring work home?"

"Yes, I told you I would. Did you bring running stuff?"

"Sure did."

They were almost done eating when his phone rang. Piper's small voice was struggling to speak through her sobs. "D-D-Daddy, d-did I leave my p-purple unicorn there?"

"Hey, hey, baby girl, let me go look. You don't need to cry like that." Sam walked toward her bedroom, talking to her softly in a soothing voice the whole time. He returned from her bedroom carrying a stuffed purple unicorn and stood next to Quinn as he set it on the counter. "Sweetie, yes, it's here. He's okay and will be right on your bed waiting for you on Monday."

"N-no, D-D-Daddy, I n-need it tonight!" Her sobbing intensified. "Mommy wants t-to talk to you."

Norah said, "I'm sorry. She's inconsolable. We'll come over there and pick it up."

Sam stepped away from Quinn and, with a note of panic in his voice, said, "No, no, you don't need to do that. I'll come to you." He continued to say he'd drive to her house, becoming more and more exasperated. Finally, Norah gave in, and he said, "I'll be there in ten minutes."

Looking at Quinn, he said. "I'm sorry. You could figure out what's going on, right?" He had grabbed his keys and was opening the door to leave.

"Yeah, she sounded so devastated."

"I appreciate you not being angry." He walked back and kissed her.

"Of course I'm not angry. We agreed I shouldn't meet Piper until we figured us out." She reached her hand up to stroke his cheek. "I gotta tell you, I loved the way you talked to her. You were so sweet."

Sam walked back in a short time later. He shook his head. "It's going to take a while to get everything figured out. She's so confused about why we're not together." He sat down next to Quinn, and she took his hand, clasping it tightly. "I hate seeing her so upset."

Quinn said, "I get it. What were Friday nights like for you before Norah left?"

"We'd have pizza and then watch a movie before we put Piper to bed. How about you? How do you spend Friday night?"

"I watch cooking competitions while drinking a glass or two of wine."

He handed her the remote. "That sounds like a nice evening. Find the right station while I pour the wine." She selected a show where the chefs had unusual ingredients with limited time to prepare a meal. They both laughed at the hectic pace while they searched on their phones to figure out what the ingredients were, competing to see who could identify them first.

After Quinn had found four in a row before him, Sam said, "I think you have an unfair advantage because you've watched before. I can't even spell most of these words."

"No, the only one I knew tonight was durian, which is some kind of fruit. Shhh, listen, the final ingredient is coming up."

They turned their attention to the television as the host announced, "Tonight's final mystery ingredient is spotted dick pudding!"

Sam burst into laughter. "Spotted what?" He tried to type on his phone, but he was laughing too hard.

Quinn's fingers were tapping on her phone, and laughter was bubbling out of her too. Sam reached over and started tickling her. She laughed harder, saying, "You're not fighting fair."

When he didn't stop, she said, "You know you won't win this." She put her hands on both sides of his ribs and started tickling him. He squirmed away until he reached the end of the couch and couldn't escape any further.

Quinn was relentless and didn't stop until Sam managed to say, through his laughter, "Uncle, uncle, I give up."

She sat back with a look of satisfaction. "You were always more ticklish than me."

When Sam caught his breath, he said, "God, it felt good to laugh like that. Thank you."

Quinn reached her hands toward his rib cage again and said, "I can keep going."

Sam caught her hands, pulled her on top of him, and murmured, "No," just before pressing his lips to hers. Her mouth opened, and his tongue explored as Quinn moaned. Her hands slid under his shirt, stroking his back.

Quinn sat up, pulling Sam along with her. They stood and embraced tightly. He said, "I'm not sure what your expectations are."

"I'm not sure either."

Sam nodded his head toward the hall. "Bedroom?"

Just as Quinn nodded, her phone rang with a distinctive ringtone. "Hold that thought. It's my friend Ashley. I need to take this."

"Hey, what's up?" She put the phone on speaker so Sam could hear.

"I'm so sorry to call you, but we are critically short for the eleven-to-seven shift. Is there any chance you can come back in? I've tried everyone I can think of."

Quinn answered, "None of the per diems are available?" Ashley answered that she'd tried them all.

Quinn looked at Sam. "I can't say no."

He mouthed, *Do what you have to do.*

"I can cover, but you need to know I had a glass of wine earlier."

"Only one glass? How long ago? I've never seen you incapacitated by one glass of wine."

"Yeah, just one, and it was more than an hour ago, so by the time I get there, I'll be fine. I'll be in as soon as I can, but I'm not at my house, so it'll be a bit of time."

"You're a lifesaver! See you soon."

Sam grinned at her. "So, this is what it's like being involved with a nurse?"

She nodded. "It happens once in a while. I'll need to sleep after the shift, so I'll go to my place and come here after I get up. Sorry, I'll miss running with you."

"We'll make it a late-afternoon run. You'll be here by then?"

"Should be."

After she left, Sam crawled into bed, turned off the light, rolled over, and pounded the pillow. *Dammit, I really wanted to sleep with her in my arms, even if we didn't have sex.*

Chapter Five

Memories

QUINN ARRIVED AT SAM's house midafternoon dressed in running clothes. "I'm a lot slower than you are."

He hugged her. "That's okay. We'll do a nice, easy run. I missed you last night. I was looking forward to sleeping with you in my arms."

They ran along a dirt road which saw very little traffic. Most of the foliage had fallen off the trees. Only the golden tamarack trees gave color to the landscape. They veered away from the road onto a path through the woods, where their feet kicked through the piles of crisp, faded leaves on the ground. They were both sweaty and breathing hard when Sam stopped and said, "Do you recognize this place?"

He watched as Quinn looked around. She shook her head. "I feel like I should, but I don't."

"This is where the state cross-country championships are held. Do you remember you came to see me run here my senior year? We'd only known each other a couple of months."

Recognition lit her eyes. "I remember that! I begged my mother to bring me down here so I could watch my friend run. She had no idea who my friend was."

"My parents never came to any of my races. That was the first time I'd had someone cheering me on. It was huge for me. Your friendship meant so much." He put his arms around her. "That's what I've missed so much all these years."

He kissed her gently. "The way your parents took me in was life-changing for me. Cheering for me at ski meets before they even knew who I was and letting me stay at your house after I left for college. I told you in Boston what a huge role that played in showing me the kind of life I wanted."

It was obvious she was blinking back tears. He'd talked a little in Boston about how he seldom saw his parents, but Sam was sure she'd forgotten how terrible his relationship with them, particularly his father, had been. It was one reason he had spent so much time at her house.

Quinn touched his cheek. "I've missed our friendship too. You said in Boston that your relationship with your folks is still fractured?"

"Yeah, I see very little of them. It's easier to stay away than get tangled up in my father's black moods. I miss my brothers, but we all grew apart. Matt still lives near them, and remember I told you Joe is in Boston? They've only seen Piper a handful of times. But hey, that's not why we ran this way. I only wanted to see if you remembered that meet. We should head back."

Sam showered first, and when he heard Quinn turn off the shower, he called from the kitchen, "I forgot to buy soy sauce. I'm going to run to the mini-mart."

Quinn walked into the kitchen wrapped in a towel. "Give me a minute, and I'll go with you."

Sam opened his eyes wide at the sight of her. He walked over and wrapped his arms around her, nuzzling her neck. "You make me not want to leave. I won't be long. Take your time getting dressed. I'll probably be back before you're done."

After dinner, they watched a movie and spent more time making out than they had the night before. They went to sleep entangled in each other's arms.

Sam woke up in the middle of the night to find Quinn lazily stroking his cock. His mouth curled into a smile as he relished the feel of her hand on his erection. It reminded him of the times they spent together as teenagers before they started having sex. There were many nights she had brought him to a climax with her hand. Tonight, while one hand stroked his cock, the other sought his nipple. Her fingers traced circles before pinching him, which brought a moan from Sam.

His pelvis moved against her hand, urging her to go faster, but instead, she slowed down and found his lips with her mouth. His mouth was open, and her tongue plunged inside. She explored his mouth before tracing kisses down his neck until her lips reached his nipple and sucked on it.

Her stroking increased in speed as Sam moaned and thrust against her. He shuddered, and the stickiness of his climax exploded over both of them. Quinn's hand moved to her clit. Sam rolled toward her and snaked his hand between her legs. He felt her wetness and drove two fingers into her, causing an explosive orgasm. She moaned softly as his fingers moved while the waves continued wracking her.

After their heartbeats returned to normal, Sam went to the bathroom and returned with a warm washcloth, which he gently ran over her stomach and between her legs. He placed it on the floor and crawled onto the mattress, spooning against her again. Neither of them had said a word.

Sam woke up first, with his arms still wrapped around her. He worked his hands under her T-shirt, searching for her breasts. He cupped one, and her breathing remained even. His erection pressed against her back as he increased his touch on her breast. She shifted, pressing her back against him. After finding her other breast, he pinched the nipple, making her jump and roll over to face him.

Their lips smashed together, and his tongue drove inside her mouth. Her hand moved down his back and briefly stroked his butt before moving to his cock. His mouth moved away from hers, and he kissed his way to her breast. Taking it in his mouth, he sucked hard while Quinn pushed against him. Sam could tell she wanted more as she gripped his hand, guiding it to her other breast and moaning as his fingers pinched her nipple.

Her breath was coming fast, and Sam could feel the frenzied beating of her heart. There was a box of condoms beside the mattress, and he quickly rolled one over his erection before returning to Quinn's breasts while his hand slid between her legs. She was slick with desire, and Sam fingered her as he had a few hours earlier. Rolling onto her back, Quinn pulled him on top of her. His cock slid in easily, and her mouth found his nipple. He pushed hard and fast, coming on the fourth stroke. Groaning, he softly murmured, "Norah."

He was still breathing hard as Quinn rolled away from him and went into the bathroom. *Fuck! Where the hell did that come from?*

He walked to the bathroom door. "Babe, are you okay?" There was no sound, and after what seemed like forever, Sam tried again. "Quinn, I'm sorry, please talk to me."

She walked out, and he gathered her into a hug. "I'm so sorry I left you behind. You turned me on so much I lost control. And then you left. I would have gotten you there. I want it to be great for you."

Her arms were at her side, and she was like a statue against him. She spit out, "I'm not bothered by the lack of orgasm. You called out Norah's name!"

He backed away from her and looked into her eyes. "I'm so sorry. I don't know where that came from."

"Did you think that's who was in bed with you?"

"No, no, no, not at all." He rubbed his hand over his jaw. "Can you forgive me?"

She ignored his question. "I need a shower."

"I'll make breakfast while you do that, and then we can talk. Quinn, you're the only one I want to be with."

He went to the kitchen but could still hear the shower. She was in the bathroom for a long time, and he couldn't imagine what was going through her mind. Breakfast and coffee were waiting on the island when Quinn finally walked out to the kitchen. She took a long drink of the coffee before looking at him. "I need to go home."

His face crumpled. "What can I say to make you stay? In Boston, we agreed to see where this could go. You don't want to do that now? Because of one word I said?"

"It wasn't just a word, Sam. It's the mother of your child, the woman you were living with until a couple of weeks ago." She pushed the plate away. "I need to think. I will not make a decision while I'm feeling this emotional."

"Please stay so we can talk it out."

"I can't. Do you know how demeaning that was? To have you call out another woman's name while your cock was buried inside me? I'm humiliated."

"You know I didn't mean to hurt you. I was with Norah for a long time. It's a reflex, like muscle memory."

"I don't know anything right now." Sam trailed behind as Quinn walked back to the bedroom and picked up her bag.

"Is this it, then? I'm never going to see you again?" His despair came through loud and clear.

"I'm not saying that." She took a deep breath. "I promised you no recriminations if we decide this doesn't work, but I'm too angry and too hurt to decide anything today. I need some time."

"Piper will be here tomorrow and Tuesday. Can we get together on Wednesday?" He reached for her hand. "Please believe me—I do not want to be with Norah. Since I sat next to you, I have been happier than I'd been in years. I..." He took a deep breath. "I love... spending time with you."

"I can't promise when I'll be ready to talk."

Sam nodded. "I'm really sorry, Quinn."

"I know."

After Quinn left, Sam sat in the living room, considering the long day stretching before him. He thought they'd have all day together and had pictured watching her study the same way he did when she was in high school. He had hoped they'd spend more time in bed. Now the whole damn day loomed, with nothing to do.

He grabbed his keys and drove to the nearby mini-mart to buy a twelve pack of beer. He'd gotten drunk in Boston the night he told Quinn about Norah leaving and felt so crappy the next day that he told Quinn he didn't know when he'd drink like that again. Well, now he knew. He was going to get drunk today.

Chapter Six
A Sad Goodbye

SAM SURVIVED MONDAY AND Tuesday by keeping busy with his job during the day and Piper at night. He had sent Quinn several texts but only received responses to a few of them. Quinn let him know she'd come to his house after work on Wednesday, and he was afraid of what was going to happen.

He'd been on edge all day and didn't open the garage door. Instead, he stood in the doorway, waiting for her. Quinn climbed slowly out of the car and walked toward him with her head bowed. Sam knew it was to avoid facing his eyes. He held the door open and followed her in then said, "Let's sit on the couch." He sat at the opposite end from her. She finally looked at him, and he said, "I'm not going to like what you say, am I?"

She said with a sad smile, "No." After taking a deep breath and blowing it out, she said, "I can't do this. I've known all along, but I let myself get caught up by the memories and incredible sex. You're not over Norah."

He protested, "I am. We haven't gotten along in years. I don't want to live like that anymore. She did me a favor by moving out."

"You had me park in your garage, you won't go to a restaurant with me, and you won't let me go grocery shopping with you. You're afraid Norah's going to find out you're seeing me. I'm not interested in a relationship where we sneak around, where I have to be hidden."

"It's not like that."

"Really? Because I've done a lot of thinking since Sunday, and it seems exactly like that." Her voice was harsh.

"We're still working things out, like time with Piper. I'm afraid if Norah finds out I'm seeing you, it will screw things up. So yeah, I guess we are sneaking around, but it won't be like this forever. We'll get those things nailed down, and then I'll be free to do what I want."

"But you admit you're not at that point right now. We should have waited."

"We spent ten years apart. I didn't realize how much I missed you until I saw you again. Your friendship meant everything to me back then, and it means everything to me right now. We wasted so much time. I want to be with you. Christ, I'm sorry

I said Norah's name the other night. If I hadn't done that, we wouldn't be having this conversation."

"Maybe we wouldn't be having it tonight, but we would have it sometime." She shook her head. "In Boston, you admitted you'd never been alone and that you needed to learn to do that. I've stepped in, and you're right back where you've always been, not making any progress toward being independent. You said you haven't even thought about the house or getting some furniture. We talked about codependency in Boston. My God, you're the definition of it! You're texting me all the time, and you've asked me to stay every night that Piper isn't here." She tented her hands and touched her lips. "I've worked hard to become self-sufficient. I enjoy my own company and time by myself."

"You can have time for yourself."

"Oh, thank you so much! I didn't know I needed your permission."

"I didn't mean it like that. We won't see each other on the days Piper is here. I don't expect us to be together all the time. We talked about that."

"Sam, you're sending me twenty or more text messages every day! Even when you have Piper. And even after I asked you not to do that. You're acting like you did when we were teenagers!"

"I'll stop."

"We both know that's not true. I'm grateful for our time in Boston. I've been stuck as far as relationships go, and learning the truth about what you said to me ten years ago has made me feel better about myself. You said you've always regretted the way things ended. Now the slate is clean. It's an opportunity to move forward for both of us, but not together. Have you seen Jesse since we were in Boston?"

"Why? What does that have to do with us?"

"Have you seen him?"

Sam shook his head. "No, I haven't seen him."

"I thought you were going to have dinner with his family last week?"

Guilt flitted across his face as he realized what she was saying.

"You saw me instead, didn't you?" He nodded. "Sam, this is what I mean! You're directing all your energy toward me. It's not healthy!"

"I thought I was putting my energy toward us! I love you!"

"No, no, no, please don't say that."

"Why not? It's true. I loved you ten years ago, and I love you now!" Agitated, he slid over to sit next to her, taking her hands in his. "We can make this work!"

"I don't feel the same way."

"I don't believe you. All the conversations and the attraction. You want me as much as I want you."

"Sam, I can't deny how much I enjoyed spending time with you in Boston. The physical attraction is over the top, but that's not enough. I don't love you, and I cannot continue to see you.

It's not good for either of us." She pulled her hands out of his and stood up.

He stood as well and said, "I can't change your mind, can I?" She shook her head. Putting his hands on her shoulders, he said, "I'm going to take care of all that we've talked about—Norah, fear of being alone, codependency, all of it. And I'm going to come back to you, the new and improved me."

"I hope you do all those things, but don't do it for me, do it for yourself. Don't close yourself off to other women because you think I'm going to be there. Find a whole new healthy relationship." After a hesitation, she added, "This needs to be a clean break. Please don't keep texting me. I won't reply."

"You said you wanted to be friends no matter what happened. Are you taking that back?"

"No. I want us to be friends, but for right now, I think we need space between us. Work on all those things you mentioned without me in the picture."

She moved toward the door, and just before she walked out, he put his arms around her, drawing her close to him. She leaned into him briefly and whispered, "Be happy."

Sam stood rooted in the same spot, watching her drive away from his life.

He watched until her car was out of sight then slowly closed the door and grabbed the beer he had opened earlier. Settling on the couch, he drained the can and put it on the floor then leaned his head back and felt the tears flowing from his eyes. He angrily wiped them away, but they kept coming. He hadn't shed a tear over Norah leaving, but now, when faced with the loss of Quinn, he couldn't stop crying.

Chapter Seven

Dinner With Jesse

A WEEK LATER, SAM drove over the Connecticut River on his way to Wednesday-night dinner with Jesse and Caitlin. *Thank God they realized what a hard time I'd have without Norah and Piper around. I can't spend another night by myself. Having Piper with me over the weekend kept me going, but I won't have her again until Monday.* The prospect of five nights alone was daunting.

Quinn's words had reverberated through his mind since she drove away a week ago. And as much as he hated it to admit it, he knew she was right. He needed to get himself together.

He glanced at the river, looking for the rowers as he and Piper had done that first weekend. *I was happy on that drive. And now I'm... what am I?* Tears filled his eyes as they had several times since Quinn had broken off what he'd hoped was their budding second chance at a relationship. *I'm lost.*

Sam continued past the popular strip malls as his emotions spiraled out of control. Seeing a rest area, he pulled in, killed the ignition, and climbed out of his car. He drew a deep, shuddering breath and angrily wiped his eyes then took several deep breaths and looked around, realizing this was the same rest area he had stopped at after Norah told him she was moving out. *This is worse. Losing Quinn a second time is hitting in such a different way than losing Norah.*

Climbing back into the car, Sam continued toward his friend's house, relieved that the long drive would give him time to pull himself together. Spending time with Jesse would help, too, as it always did.

His friendship with Jesse had begun when they shared an office years before, and even after Jesse completed his advanced degree and started his own consulting firm, they had remained close friends. Jesse had been the first to recognize Norah's attraction to Sam when she worked on a project with them. As Norah and Sam's relationship had grown, they'd formed a strong bond with Jesse and Caitlin.

As Sam thought about that, he grimaced, realizing Norah's departure could have ramifications on his connection with the Ortegas. *No! Jesse and I were friends first—that will not change.*

Sam began to relax for the first time in days as he turned into Jesse's driveway and saw him tossing a baseball with his twelve-year-old son, Diego. As soon as Sam stepped out of his car, Diego threw the ball his way.

Sam grabbed it barehanded out of the chilly air. "Shouldn't this be a football?" he asked, even though he knew the answer. Diego was crazy about baseball and wanted to play year-round.

"I'm trying to convince Mom and Dad to move back to Florida." Diego caught Sam's throw. "I can't even remember living there. If I'm going to make the major leagues, that's where I need to be." Diego tossed the ball to his father. "Do you know how many New Englanders make it to the big leagues? Almost none. My career prospects are being hampered here."

Sam looked toward Jesse, who rolled his eyes. Diego had been making this argument for years, as he wanted to follow in his father's footsteps. Jesse had played professional baseball until an injury cut his career short. He and his wife Caitlin moved to New England after that injury, to be near her family.

Jesse and Sam continued tossing the ball with Diego for a few minutes until Jesse said, "Can't put it off any longer, buddy. You need to go inside and get started on your homework."

Diego grumbled but did not argue. Jesse and Sam followed him into the house, making their way to the game room.

"He doesn't let up, huh?" Sam smirked. "Should I expect that kind of single-mindedness from Piper when she gets to the teenage years?"

"God, I don't know. Diego isn't even a teen yet." Jesse handed Sam a beer. "This has been going on since he was eight. Toni's ten now, but she doesn't go after us about anything like he does." He took a swallow of his beer. "Kids! What are you going to do?"

"Piper's the best thing in my life right now." Sam's voice had gone thick with emotion, and he turned to the rack of pool cues as he fought to compose himself. Beside the rack, he noticed a new picture of Jesse and his family on top of Mount Washington. "Did you climb Washington? I want to, but I didn't think Piper was ready during the summer." Jesse's daughter Janey was the same age as Piper.

"No, we took the Cog," Jesse answered, referring to the train that traveled to the summit of New England's highest peak. "Janey's too small. Maybe she and Piper will be ready in a couple of years, and we can all do it together." He paused and looked at Sam. "How are you doing?"

Sam took a deep breath as he removed two cues from the rack. "Honestly, not great." He handed one cue to Jesse. "You can break."

After Jesse had scattered the balls, Sam lined up his first shot. "Norah took all the furniture. Number one in the corner." When the ball went in the hole, he studied the table for a minute before walking to the other side. "She thinks it's visitation when I have Piper. Number two in the center pocket." He moved a few inches for his third shot. "She's taking Pip to Connecticut for Thanksgiving. Number three in the center." The ball sailed past the hole and careened into the corner of the table. "Your turn."

"You're still pissed," Jesse said, sounding a little surprised. "It's been a few weeks. I thought you'd have that under control." Jesse took a shot that missed by inches. He winced as he backed away from the table.

"What's up with you?" Sam studied Jesse. "You're limping more than usual."

"I hiked Mount Lafayette with Janey's class yesterday." He grimaced. "One of the boys sprained his ankle. Two moms and I alternated carrying him down the mountain." He rubbed his leg. "I hate to admit it, but I'm hurting."

"Geesh, why didn't you say something? Let's sit." Sam took the cue from him and put it back on the rack. They walked over to the fireplace, which Jesse turned on before stretching out in the recliner. Sam sat on the other one and grinned. "Ooh, we're going to be romantic with a fire, huh?"

"You asshole. I'm freezing. Diego had me out there for an hour before you arrived. He could be right about Florida. We've been here ten years, and I still don't like the cold."

"Right. Move to Florida." Sam sighed. "Just what I need, my best friend abandoning me."

"Don't worry. It's not going to happen. That's not the environment we want to raise the kids in." Jesse finished his beer. "So, Norah took all the furniture?"

Sam nodded. He walked to the fridge, took out two more bottles, and held one out to Jesse, who shook his head. Sam put one bottle back and took a long drink from the other. "But the worst thing? She left me a fucking *note!*"

"A note?"

"Yeah. It had her new address and a couple of sentences about how this had to happen, but at the end it implied..." Sam shook his head. "I don't know what she was trying to say. Her lease is only for six months. What does she think is going to change?" He sighed and looked at Jesse. "She ended it saying she'd always love me, but there was no sign of love the next day. All I know is I'm done."

"That's how it's been all along, isn't it? Push and pull, hot and cold?"

"Yeah." Sam shrugged. "But what's going on with your leg? Are you going to get it looked at?"

Jesse matched Sam's shrug. "I overdid it. Carrying that kid down the mountain was too much, but I couldn't be an able-bodied man and let these two women do it all."

"Except you're not able-bodied." Sam knew the extent of Jesse's injury and how many surgeries he'd had, knew Jesse'd had to overcome a brief addiction to painkillers. He knew it all.

"Thanks for the reminder. I'll be fine in a couple of days. What about Quinn? Did you get all that crap you've been carrying around for ten years off your chest?"

Sam started playing with the label on his bottle. He remembered the feel of Quinn's body against his, her hand wrapped around his cock, and the staggering orgasms they'd shared. Then how she had told him that trying to be together again was a mistake. He shook his head to clear his thoughts.

"It took several beers, but I told her where my shitty behavior came from. I was relieved to have it out in the open. We talked about a lot of things. I think it helped both of us." He studied the label, fully aware of Jesse staring at him. He looked up, meeting his friend's eyes. "What!"

"Nothing. I've never seen you blush before." Jesse grinned.

"We saw each other a couple of times at my house."

"Holy crap. You got laid, didn't you?" Jesse cackled.

"It wasn't like that."

"Sorry." Jesse raised his hands in surrender. "You're really upset, aren't you? And this goes beyond Norah."

Sam nodded. "The sex was epic, but more than that, being with Quinn was so easy, exactly like it was when we dated before. She put an end to it a few days ago because she thinks I'm not over Norah." He stretched his arms over his head. "She's probably right. I want to be, but I'm not."

Sam was considering telling Jesse what happened the last time Quinn was at his house, when Antonia, Jesse's middle child, clattered down the stairs and burst into the room. "Mom says dinner is ready." She held up her right hand. "Hi, Sam."

Sam stood and high-fived her. "Hey, Toni." He reached a hand to Jesse. "Want some help, old man?"

Jesse frowned, but Sam could tell he appreciated the assist.

When the three of them reached the top of the stairs, a miniature version of Antonia hurled herself at Sam. "Why didn't you bring Piper with you?" Janey demanded as he caught her up in his arms. She continued to hang on Sam's neck as he walked toward the dining room, where he peeled her off, marveling as he always did at the resemblance between Jesse's two daughters. Janey, the dynamo who had latched onto him, was one of Piper's best friends. "Is she home with Norah? I want to play with her! She should have come!"

Sam chuckled and put her down. "We'll set up something soon. But not on a school night."

"You kids need to give me a chance to say hello to Sam." Caitlin reached out, and he gathered her into a hug. "I'm sorry about Norah," she whispered in his ear.

"Have you talked to her?" Sam asked.

"A few times." Caitlin looked uncomfortable.

"I won't ask you to betray her trust."

"I know you won't." She started to turn then paused. "None of this was easy for her."

As soon as they were seated at the table, all three kids started talking at the same time, each vying for the adults' attention. Their parents made them take turns, and Diego told them about a science project he was working on.

On Toni's turn, she said, "I have to pick out the winter sport to do after Christmas, and I want to try skiing instead of skating."

"I'm going to ski this winter." Sam smiled. "Maybe we can go together some weekend."

"I wanna ski." Janey pouted. "I never get to do anything fun."

"Where will you ski, Sam?" Caitlin asked.

"Near where I grew up. It's about an hour north of my house." Sam paused. "You could all try it. My whole family skied when I was a kid."

Janey pounced on that. "Can we please, pretty please?"

Jesse and Caitlin looked at each other.

Sam winked at the kids. "They're going to say, 'We'll see.' It's the universal parent answer. I use it all the time with Piper."

After the kids left the table, the three adults lingered.

Jesse eyed Sam. "What made you decide to ski this winter?"

"Quinn asked me about it, and it made me realize how much I miss it."

"Quinn?" Caitlin cocked her head at Sam.

"A girl I dated in another lifetime. I ran into her at that conference in Boston."

"Oh."

"I'm sure Norah has mentioned her to you." When Caitlin nodded, Sam grimaced. "Quinn's kind of a sore point for us."

"I'm aware of that. It seems irrational after all the time you and Norah have been together."

"*Irrational* is a good word for it." Sam scoffed.

Jesse leaned forward. "You know I'll never be able to ski."

Sam was happy about the change of topic. "You might be okay on the beginner slope with Janey. Or you can sit in the lodge and enjoy an adult beverage. I'd be happy to ski with her."

"It pisses me off that this"—he motioned to his rebuilt knee—"limits my life. Even now, twelve years after the fact." Jesse scowled. "That it's going to limit me forever."

Caitlin moved her chair closer to Jesse's and took his hands in hers. "You're not limited in any of the ways that matter."

Jesse sighed. "Thanks, babe." He leaned in to kiss her.

"And that's my cue to leave." Sam stood, gathered the plates, and carried them to the kitchen. "I won't even try to load your dishwasher. I'm sure I wouldn't get it right." He returned to the dining room to find Jesse and Caitlin standing, still holding hands.

They walked with Sam to the door, where Jesse put his arm over his wife's shoulder, pulling her close to him. "We're headed to Maine next week for Thanksgiving. But plan on coming for dinner again the week after."

Janey popped her head out of her bedroom. "And bring Piper!"

Diego appeared at the top of the stairs. "Hey, Sam, bring your glove next time."

"Make me a list of what I'll need for skiing!" Toni called. "Please."

Sam grinned. "I don't know if I can remember all that." He kissed Caitlin on the cheek. "Dinner was delicious. Happy Thanksgiving."

In the car, Sam thought about how much he enjoyed spending time with Jesse's family. As the road unwound in front of him, he realized he felt better than he had in weeks. And a long-buried thought bubbled to the surface.

I want more kids.

Chapter Eight

Thanksgiving Festival

As Piper wrapped her arms around him at the entrance to the multipurpose room at Chelford Elementary School, Sam's heart overflowed with love for his daughter. She led him into the room for the school's Thanksgiving dinner, and when the aroma of roast turkey reached Sam's nose, his stomach growled.

Fall decor of cornstalks, bales of hay, and bright-orange pumpkins adorned the room, and at the center of each table was a cornucopia with fruit and gourds spilling out of it. The feast was an annual event to mark the start of Thanksgiving break. Kids were streaming through the door on the opposite side of the room, jostling to find the correct table for their classroom. Pip directed him to the chair next to Norah.

As he pulled it out to sit, Norah stopped him. "Pip, you sit there. Daddy can sit on the other side, then we'll both be close to you."

Smooth, Norah, real smooth. I don't want to sit next to you either. This saves us from having to pretend that everything is fine. Sam slid over, leaving the chair empty between him and Norah.

Before Piper sat down, she started waving at a silver-haired man talking to a woman Sam didn't recognize. "Mr. D-D-Donovan, Mr. D-D-Donovan."

Sam watched a smile blossom on Scott Donovan's face. As the head of speech-language pathology at the school, Scott had worked with Piper quite a bit.

When Mr. Donovan and the auburn-haired woman reached the table, Piper said, "Look at the p-p-place cards. We m-made them in art c-c-class."

"I like them." Scott admired the cards then motioned to the woman by his side. "This is Sophie Palmer. She's the sub for Ms. Thomas until mid-January."

"Ms. Thomas is going to have a b-baby!" Piper told her parents.

"Yes, she is." Scott smiled. "These kids don't miss a thing. She needs to rest for a few weeks, so Ms. Palmer will fill in for her. Sophie, this is Norah Taylor and Sam Carpenter. They're the lucky folks who get to be Pip's parents."

Norah spoke first, shaking Sophie's outstretched hand. "It's nice to meet you. Will you be working with Piper?"

"No," Scott answered for her. "She'll be working with the middle grades."

"Oh." Norah's face fell. "I thought maybe someone new…"

"Not that we're unhappy with you, Mr. Donovan," Sam cut in.

"I understand." Scott frowned. "We're going to find the answer, I promise you."

Just then, another child called to the genial man, and Sophie grinned at Scott. "You're popular."

Norah nodded. "He's great."

"My fame is greatly exaggerated. I hope you all have a wonderful Thanksgiving." Scott fist-bumped Piper as he turned to lead Sophie to the other tables to make introductions.

For the first time since Norah had moved out, Sam felt a hint of compassion for her. He had seen her excitement over the possibility of a new SPL and shared her disappointment, but he also hoped Norah's insinuation that someone new might be more successful didn't offend Mr. Donovan. It wasn't the first time her bluntness had made Sam squirm.

During the dinner, Piper jabbered at both of them while they ate, telling Sam how excited she was to see her cousins in Connecticut. She had always been a chatterbox, and the stutter had not changed that. "What are you g-going to do on Thanksgiving, D-D-Daddy?"

"I'm going to have dinner with my parents and my brothers."

Norah frowned when Sam mentioned his family, and Piper looked confused.

"Your brothers?" Piper asked.

"You may not remember them. We don't see them often. But yes, I have brothers just like Mommy has a brother and two sisters."

"D-d-do I have more cousins?"

"No, neither of them has children."

Piper still looked bewildered, and Sam's dismay grew as he realized she didn't know he had a family.

When lunch finished, the school principal dismissed the students for Thanksgiving break, and Piper gripped Sam's hand as they walked to Norah's car.

When he opened the door, Piper wrapped her arms around his legs. "I wish you were coming with us, D-D-Daddy," she said, tears trembling behind her voice.

Sam kneeled to hug her, and tears soaked his shirt as she buried her face in his shoulder. "Mommy," she managed through her sobs, "c-can't D-Daddy come with us? Please?"

Sam looked up at Norah, sure that Piper's pleas would gut her the same way they were him, but he saw no emotion.

"Not this trip, baby girl." Norah's face and voice were calm. "Dinner will be waiting at Grandma's, so we need to leave."

Sam stood, picking Piper up with her arms still wrapped around his neck, and she clung to him before he placed her in the booster seat. "You're going to have a great time with your cousins," he promised as he buckled her in. "You can tell me all about it next week." He leaned in and kissed her forehead and her tear-damp cheeks. "I love you to the moon and back." He shut the door and walked away without a word to Norah.

Sam reached his car and turned back to watch them drive away, sagging against the car and trying to get his emotions under control. He took several deep breaths and brushed his hand over his eyes, wiping away the wetness that had threatened to spill out the minute Piper started crying.

He heard a car door open near him, so he turned. It was the red-haired woman he'd met earlier with Scott. The substitute. She seemed to be staring at him.

Well, this is awkward. Here I am in the school parking lot, falling apart.

He took a deep breath. "Hi, Ms.—um, I'm sorry, but I don't remember your name."

"Sophie."

"Ms. Sophie?"

"Just Sophie. Are you okay?"

"Yeah." Sam rubbed his jaw then shrugged. "Actually, no. My daughter's leaving with her mother for Thanksgiving break. They're going to be in Connecticut all weekend. I don't like being separated from her."

"Your daughter is Piper, right? She's adorable. I loved her pigtails."

He nodded. *Okay, I'm impressed. She stood at the table for a minute and remembers us. Wait, is that good or bad? Did we stand out because of the hostility between us?*

"Is work keeping you here?" Sophie asked.

Sam shrugged again. "Actually, we're not living together."

Sophie clapped her hand over her mouth. "I'm sorry. It's none of my business."

"The separation is new, just a couple of weeks. Only a few people know. Although..." He paused. "I think Norah told Scott. Pip stutters. We think it's a reaction to the tension between us."

Sophie nodded. "I heard the stutter, and it's good for Mr. Donovan to know. Family issues can contribute."

"Yeah." Sam sighed. "Well, nice to meet you. Hope you have a happy Thanksgiving."

"You too."

Sam opened his car door. "Hey, thanks for noticing the pigtails. It took a lot of practice to get them right."

An unfamiliar feeling sparked in his chest. Happiness? Gratitude? Whatever it was, he didn't feel it enough. *I like that.* He slid into his car, smiling as he thought about Sophie's appreciation of Piper's pigtails.

Chapter Nine

Return to the Whistle Stop

SAM SAT IN HIS parents' driveway, thinking about the last time he'd been there and what a disaster it had been. Since then, he had only come north, only seen his family, when there was a gathering at his grandparents' or his aunt's house. He took a deep breath before he climbed out of the car, wondering if his father had started drinking.

Sam's mom opened the door, and he handed her the vase filled with fall flowers he had purchased the day before. She set it down in the entryway and gave him a hug.

He held her tightly for a moment, unable to recall the last time they had hugged like this. He needed it.

When they parted, he looked around. Big changes in the house were apparent from his vantage point. "You've done some major remodeling."

Joe arrived in time to hear Sam's comment. "Can I show him around, Ma?" He gathered her into a warm hug as well.

She smiled. "Of course! You handled most of the work."

As they walked around the house, Joe pointed out the changes that were made to the flooring and windows, plus the large addition.

Sam whistled. "Wow, did you and Dad do all of this?"

"They hired someone for the addition, but we did all the finish work. I was at loose ends this year and spent a lot of time here." Joe grinned. "I like the way it turned out."

"It looks amazing." Sam ran his hand over the mahogany mantel in the great room. "It would have been fantastic to have all this room when we were kids."

When they returned to the kitchen, Matt and his wife Jilly had arrived, and their dad, Trent, had appeared—and seemed to be sober, Sam noted.

They all helped get the food on the table, even Trent.

As they ate, Sam remarked again on the big changes to the house.

Joe nodded. "We should go into business—Carpenter Brothers Carpentry. You can do the design stuff, put that fancy degree of yours to work. We'd have to hire a framer, but I'd do the finish work. We'd clean up!"

Sam chuckled, "I'll design anything you want, but I think I'll hang on to my day job. I like project management."

Trent spoke up. "Joe, tell your brothers about that place you're working on north of Boston."

"Multimillion-dollar place on the north shore. Five bedrooms, six baths." Joe pulled out his phone and showed them some pictures.

"But you live in Boston, right? In the city?" Sam asked.

"Yeah. Where you were for a week and didn't even bother to call."

"I told you my time was all tied up. You drive out of the city every day? That traffic killed me."

Joe shook his head. "You need to get out of the woods more often, little brother."

"It's not that bad after you drive it a few times," Matt added.

Sam eyed Matt. "How do you know?"

"Jilly and I visit Joe. We went to one of the Bruins' playoff games last year. We've been to a few Red Sox games."

Sam rubbed his hand along his jaw, digesting that info. "I, uh, I really have been out of touch."

Laura cleared her throat. "It's a little harder for you to get away with Piper," she said, clearly defending Sam.

"Thanks, Mom," he said. "I ran through Boston Common and thought about how she'd enjoy seeing the city."

Joe raised his eyebrows. "Thought your week was tightly scheduled?"

Sam felt his face flush. "Did you want to get together at six in the morning?"

Joe shook his head and snickered. "I'm well on my way to the jobsite by then."

The conversation switched to the ski resort in town. It had new owners for the third time in fifteen years.

"They've expanded the snowmaking," Trent said. "That should help."

"I'm going to get back into skiing this year," Sam said.

"Up here?" Matt asked. When he nodded, Matt looked thoughtful. "Cool. Maybe I will too. We can race. It'll be like old times."

As they ate dessert, Matt cleared his throat loudly. "We have something to tell you all," he said and took a breath. "We're going to have a baby. Jilly's in her seventeenth week, so we think it's going to happen this time."

Laura had kept Sam up-to-date about their struggles to have a child. Jilly'd had three miscarriages, the last one a year ago at nine weeks.

"I'm sorry we didn't tell you sooner," Matt continued. "We've been superstitious about telling anyone this time." He took Jilly's hand.

Laura hugged Jilly with tears in her eyes. "I didn't think when I mentioned Sam having Piper before. I'm sorry. But I am so happy for you! You're going to have a baby!"

Jilly hugged her back. "It's okay. You didn't say it intentionally. And I know having a child will change everything. We can't wait!"

Trent shook Matt's hand as Joe and Sam added their congratulations, and dinner ended on a high note. The boys left for camp a short time later, Matt joining Sam and Joe since Laura, Jilly, and Jilly's mother were going to Burlington for Black Friday shopping until Saturday.

The camp's appearance stunned Sam as he approached. *Holy shit! Joe told me they'd done some work on it, but I wasn't expecting this.* He looked up at the two-story addition at the back of the cabin.

When Joe walked up behind him, Sam turned to his brother. "Dude, this looks like you pounded a lot of nails! I didn't realize that you'd done something this big."

Joe beamed. "I wanted to see your reaction. I convinced Dad we should turn this into a vacation rental. None of us hunt anymore, and if we want to, we can go to Uncle John's place. This is such a pretty spot, so close to the mountain and with the stream right there. It's been a fun project, but we're not done yet."

Originally, the cabin had a living room, bedroom, and a tiny kitchen. An outhouse in the woods had served as the bathroom, and the heat source had been a small wood stove. The addition gave it a gourmet kitchen, a bathroom, and another bedroom on the first floor, plus a large bedroom and bath on the second floor. The walls had been insulated and a heat pump installed. There was a stone fireplace in the living room, very similar to the one Sam had built in his house.

Joe proudly showed Sam all the work he'd done with Trent. "It'll be next year before it's all finished. The second floor is still rough, though, and that's what I want your help with this weekend."

Sam swiveled his head in amazement, trying to take in all the changes. "You've done a great job. I'm impressed."

"It always had a strong spring for water, and we put in a septic system," Joe continued before he began describing what still needed to be done. "We will landscape next year, and we need to upgrade the furniture. I'm hoping we'll be ready to offer it for rent during the foliage season."

They spent the evening playing gin rummy for a quarter a game. Matt was the big winner, and Joe told him to use the money to start a savings account for the baby.

"You guys can't believe how nervous I am about this pregnancy," Matt admitted. "I don't know if Jilly will survive another miscarriage."

Sam nodded. "But seventeen weeks is good, right? The other pregnancies haven't gone this far, have they?"

"No, just shy of ten weeks. And she feels differently this time. The morning sickness was terrible until a couple of weeks ago. That's never happened before, so we're hoping it's a good sign."

"Piper will be excited to have a new cousin."

Matt smiled. "You need to have another one. Piper needs a sibling."

Sam looked away. "Unlikely." He stood. "It's late, and I'm going to hit the hay." He made his way to the bedroom.

Just before he closed the door, he heard Matt ask Joe, "Something I said?"

"Nah," Joe answered. "You know how he is about his personal life."

They spent Friday splitting and stacking firewood. After dinner that night, Matt said, "I don't want to take any more of your money tonight. Why don't we go to the Whistle Stop? There's live music on Friday night. Plus, we can play pool. I'll steal your money that way."

Whistle Stop—that was a place that brought back memories, not all of them good. "I haven't been there since I was in my early twenties." Sam grabbed his coat. "I'm game." It would be good to get out of his head for a night.

Joe drove, and as soon as they arrived, they headed for the pool tables. A server brought them beers, which were quickly downed and replaced with a second round.

A tall blonde with green eyes approached them. "If it isn't the Carpenter brothers, looking better than ever." Sam didn't recognize her. "Don't tell me you don't remember me, Joe Carpenter." The blonde was wearing a wedding ring, but a curvy brunette with brown eyes and red lips accompanied her, and Sam noticed her ring finger was bare.

Joe narrowed his eyes, a telltale sign he was trying to come up with a name. "Amy?"

Right. Sam remembered now. Joe had dated Amy Branch when he was a junior and Sam was a sophomore.

When Joe said her name, she smiled and put her arms around him. "Do you still live here?" Before Joe could answer, though, her gaze turned to the other two Carpenters. "Hey, Sam, good to see you. And, Matt, God, you were only twelve when Joe and I dated."

Sam remembered her as liking to talk. That didn't appear to have changed.

"I'm living in the Boston area, up here for Thanksgiving," Joe said. "What about you?"

"I live in Manchester. We came for the holiday as well. My husband, Caleb, is at hunting camp with my brother. My mom is spoiling the kids, so I decided we'd explore the local hotspot." Amy turned to the brunette. "This is Becca, my roommate from college. Becca, meet Joe, Sam, and Matt Carpenter. They were among the hottest of the hot boys when we were in high school, and it doesn't look like anything has changed." She grinned. "I bet I can still beat you at pool, Joe."

He chuckled. "I'll take that challenge. Rack 'em up."

Matt saw some friends and left the table to catch up with them, leaving Sam alone. He looked at Becca and motioned to an empty chair. "Looks like it's you and me." They sat down, and Sam asked, "How'd you end up here?"

"I used to come here when I was in college." Becca looked off into the distance. "I live in Portsmouth after recently splitting from my husband. He has our daughter for the weekend, and I needed a change of scene. I like Amy's family, so when she invited me for Thanksgiving, I jumped at the chance."

"I feel for you." Sam took a swig of beer. "My partner left me, too, and took our daughter to visit her family in Connecticut. How recent for you?"

"Still-reaching-for-him-in-bed recent. About two months. You?"

"Still-furious-with-her recent. A few weeks ago."

Becca grimaced. "Right before the holiday? That's cruel. How old is your daughter?"

"She's six. Yours?"

"Only three. I'm still coming to terms with being away from her on Thanksgiving for the first time." Tears sprang into her eyes. She wiped them away. "Dammit, I told myself I wouldn't do that." She shook her head. "Do you dance? I love this song."

"Yeah, I dance." Sam took her hand and led her to the dance floor just as the music changed from the song she mentioned to a ballad. Becca put her arms around Sam's neck, and he pulled her close. He couldn't remember the last time he had danced—probably at some wedding with Norah. It felt good, and he and Becca stayed on the dance floor through several songs until the band took a break.

He put his arm around Becca's waist to lead her back to the table, but she leaned in and gently kissed him before they had taken a step. Sam looked curiously at her and changed direction to go to a secluded corner, stopping first at the bar for drinks.

When they reached the table in the corner, he set down their drinks and drew Becca to him, bringing his lips to hers. At first, her response felt tentative, then she grew more passionate. They kissed for several minutes before sitting down together at the small table.

Becca picked up her glass of wine and held it before taking a long sip. "I haven't kissed another man since I met my husband."

Sam took her hand. "How long were you together.?"

"We dated for three years before we married and celebrated our fifth anniversary in July. He got involved with someone else, and I had no idea." She shook her head. "That's what hurts."

"I get that. I didn't know that Norah had rented a house and arranged for someone to move most of our furniture—all while I was at a conference in Boston. I feel incredibly stupid."

"You came home to an empty house?"

"She told me she was moving out as I was walking out the door to drive to Boston. It made for a pleasant trip."

He knew his sarcasm had hit home when Becca reached out to touch his cheek. He leaned in to kiss her again. They continued to share their stories between breaks for more kissing until the bartender announced last call.

Sam enjoyed the gentleness of Becca's touch and the passion in their kisses, but he had no desire to take it any further. Mostly, it had just felt good to give comfort and to feel comforted in return.

During a trip to the restroom, Sam overheard Matt talking to Joe. "What the fuck is Sam doing?" Matt asked. "Norah goes away for the weekend, and he plays tonsil hockey with the first woman he meets?"

"Norah's left him," Joe said. "She moved out while he was in Boston. Leave him alone."

Sam didn't stay around for the rest of their conversation. He made his way back to Becca, shaking his head.

After they finished their drinks, Sam walked her to Amy's car. "You're going to move on from reaching for him in bed. You'll kiss a second guy, then a third, and probably more."

"I'm glad you were the first." She gave him a sympathetic smile. "You're going to get over being furious."

"I know." Sam drew her into a hug, and they shared one more goodbye kiss. He walked to Joe's truck and crawled into the back seat.

Matt turned to him, frowning. "What the hell, Sam?"

"Not tonight, Matt." He closed his eyes for the ride back to camp. He wasn't sure how his head was going to handle Joe's hammer therapy the next day.

Chapter Ten

Confiding in Joe

THE NEXT MORNING, JOE was up early and cooking for all three of them. "We need to get all the Sheetrock done upstairs," he said, sliding the last of the bacon onto a plate.

Sam took another piece and nodded. He had seen the stack of Sheetrock in the second-floor bedroom when he got the tour.

"There's a crew coming on Monday for the taping," Joe continued.

"Lucky for you I came," Sam said. "No way the two of you would have gotten that done."

"I didn't schedule the tapers until I confirmed you were coming. Eat up—time's a-wasting."

They worked steadily until lunchtime, working up a sweat as they took turns wrestling the Sheetrock into place and running the nail gun.

At one point, as Sam was climbing down the ladder, Matt nudged him. "Looked pretty hot and heavy between you and Amy's friend last night."

"Knock it off," Sam said. "I'm holding a nail gun, and I'm not afraid to use it. Joe, why the hell did you decide on a cathedral ceiling?" Sam couldn't resist giving his brother a hard time, but in truth, he admired the room even if the high ceiling made the job more taxing.

Halfway through lunch, Matt asked about Norah leaving.

Sam rubbed his jaw as he sighed. "Damn, you don't stop, do you? Things have been bad for a couple of years. Piper developed a stutter. The therapist thinks it's in response to the tension between us. I moved out during the summer. Our relationship improved, and the stutter disappeared. I moved back in, and things went to hell. The stutter came back." He wiped his mouth. "Norah rented a place and moved out while I was in Boston. There, happy? Now you know the entire story."

"Sorry, I didn't mean to piss you off," Matt muttered. "I didn't know you were having problems."

Sam wondered if Matt wanted to add that if Sam had spent a little more time with his parents and siblings, they might have known what was going on. However, his brother restrained himself. Or maybe Sam was just being defensive.

Sam sighed. "I'm pissed most of the time, so it's not you. Last night with Becca was nothing. No, not nothing. We both needed it, but we wouldn't take it any further. She's hurting, I'm hurting, and last night was a pleasant diversion. Let's change the subject. I ran into Quinn when I was in Boston."

Both his brothers had known Quinn well. Matt's eyebrows rose. "Quinn Michaels? Does she still have that bangin' body?"

Sam scowled at him.

Matt grinned. "What? She had a great ass. And a rack to match. Is she living in Boston? Married? Kids?"

"She..." Sam's mind returned to the afternoon he spent with Quinn in her hotel room. He took a deep breath. "She's still got a great body. She works at Dartmouth and lives in Hanover. Single with no kids. We saw each other at the conference."

"Did you spend time with her?"

"We had dinner and caught up on our lives."

"She dated the wrong brother. I was right there in school with her." Matt and Quinn were the same age. "We could have had something great." Matt leered.

"Fuck you," Sam retorted. "Quinn chose *exactly* the right brother."

"Oh yeah? So why aren't you with her?"

Joe snorted a laugh, and Sam glared.

"Because I was a fool." Sam stood up. "Let's get back to work."

By five, they had finished the bedroom, leaving the bathroom for the next day. The three of them sat in the living room, each nursing a beer.

Matt looked at his cell. "Jilly's home. I need to head out. You'll be able to finish the bathroom without me?"

Sam looked at Joe, and they both nodded.

Matt swallowed the last of his beer and looked at Sam. "I'm sorry about you and Norah. Hopefully, you'll come to terms with it sooner rather than later." He paused. "Mom and Dad will be more understanding than you think if you tell them."

After dinner, Sam and Joe stretched out on the couches in the living room to watch football.

Sam blinked. "I'm probably going to fall asleep right here."

"Yeah, me too." Joe yawned. "Thanks for the help."

"You don't need me for design work. What you've done looks outstanding."

"Thanks. I've picked up ideas over the years. It's been fun to see it come together and make it look like I envisioned," Joe said. "I needed something to concentrate on other than how my life was going to hell."

"Right there with you. Why didn't I know this was going on?"

"I texted you a few times this year to let you know I was going to be here and asked you to come up. You always declined, or you didn't answer at all." Joe sat up, facing Sam. "You had your issues with Dad. We all did. But he's changed. It would be nice if you came around a little more often."

"Wow, both you and Matt ganging up on me about Mom and Dad." Sam grimaced. "Thanksgiving was better than I expected. Dad was on his best behavior, huh?"

Joe ran a hand through his hair, and Sam sensed he had something he wanted to say.

But when his brother remained silent, Sam went to the kitchen and brought back two beers. "I'm sorry I ignored your texts. I want to be part of this project. Piper will be with Norah every other weekend, so I could come then."

"Or you can bring her and let her spend the day with Mom while we're here. She'd love to get to know her granddaughter."

Sam sighed and thought for a minute. "I want Piper to start skiing this winter. I'm buying her skis, boots—you know, all the crap she'll need—for Christmas. It's only an hour to get here from my house, but maybe spending the weekend at Mom and Dad's when we come to ski would be possible. I'll need to come to some sort of truce with Dad to do that."

Joe nodded. "Or you can stay here."

"That'd be cool too. I'm realizing Piper needs to know all of you." Sam frowned. "What's your timeline look like?"

Joe opened an app on his phone and scrolled through the list of work left to do. "I'm taking a break until after New Year's. I have things going on in Boston that will keep me there on the weekends until Christmas. Let's work out a schedule for

January and February before we leave." He put his beer on the chest that served as a coffee table. "So... tell me more about Quinn."

"What about Quinn? We had dinner, we caught up, end of story." Sam took a swallow of his beer.

"She was at the same conference as you all week, and you only saw her one time?"

Sam looked at him but said nothing.

Joe wasn't done. "Remember, I've seen you crying in your beer over how things ended with her way back when. I find it hard to fathom you had one dinner with her and called it good. Or if that truly is what happened, you're an idiot. We both know there's shit you need to get straight with her."

When Sam didn't immediately answer, Joe raised his eyebrows comically. "Oh, that's right, your week was *tightly scheduled*. Probably no time to spend with an old girlfriend."

"Maybe you should hang out a therapist's shingle along with the design one." Sam flashed a guilty smile. "I *may* have exaggerated the schedule. We saw each other every day. The first day was dinner and catching up, which consisted of me acting like everything was fine in my life even though I was reeling."

Joe shook his head. "Jesus, Sam, you need to stop doing that."

"Yeah, my friend Jesse was at the conference and told me the same thing. So I invited Quinn to join me for a drink the next night and told her the whole miserable tale about how my life was falling apart."

"Nothing about the breakup ten years ago?"

Sam rubbed his jaw. "Oh yeah, I covered that too. Aided by copious amounts of beer, I told her everything. The conversation was good for both of us. Made me realize some changes I need to make. She told me hearing that the breakup wasn't all her fault helped her come to peace with it. We..." He stopped. Did he want to share the fact that they'd had sex? And tried to rekindle things?

"You..." Joe gestured, urging him to continue.

Sam took a deep breath. "We took it to bed the last night. Intended it to be a onetime thing." He smiled at the memory. "But then we spent the next afternoon together, and it was epic. We decided to see each other back here in the real world, but that didn't last long." He sighed, remembering Quinn's goodbye.

"Not your choice, I gather."

"No, I fucked up big time. We had sex at my house..." He finished his beer and stared at the can. Finally, lifting his eyes to look at Joe, he admitted, "I called out Norah's name."

Joe's eyes widened. "Ouch."

"Yeah, Quinn took a few days to think about it, but she ended up telling me that us trying to be together was a mistake, that I wasn't over Norah, no matter what I said."

"I take it that's not sitting well with you."

Sam took another deep breath. "No, but there's stuff I need to work out. Do you realize I've never lived on my own? I need to learn to do that. And Quinn doesn't need a rebound relationship."

"Who are you trying to convince?" Joe asked, cocking his head.

"Quinn drove the conversation, and I didn't like it, but truthfully, she's right. Losing her a second time hurts even more than Norah moving out, and... son of a bitch, I've wanted to call her every single day."

Joe shrugged. "I got no words of wisdom for you on that one."

"Yeah. I'm a fucking mess."

The next morning, to Sam's relief, their conversation centered on the work at the cabin. Shortly after noon, all the Sheetrock was up in the bathroom.

As they were getting ready to leave, Sam asked Joe, "What time will Dad leave camp?"

"He's probably home now. Doesn't stay in the woods as long as he used to," Joe said. "Why?"

"You and Matt wore me down. I'm going to stop there on my way home, tell them about Norah."

Joe fist-bumped him. "I'm glad. This has been a good weekend. I've missed hanging out like this."

"Me, too, although I didn't realize how much. Anyway, I had a much better weekend than I expected." He smiled. "Stay in touch. I promise I'll respond."

When Sam pulled into his parents' driveway later that day, his mom opened the door before he got out of his car. "We didn't expect to see you again. Is everything okay?"

He gave her a quick hug. "Everything is fine." He followed her into the great room where his father was watching the Patriots. *How much has he had to drink?*

Trent raised a hand in greeting.

Sam sat in one of the chairs. His leg bounced nervously. "Sorry to interrupt the game."

Trent waved his hand at the television dismissively. "Don't worry about it. The Pats are way ahead with two minutes to play. It's not every day you stop by." He smiled at Laura, who had joined him on the couch.

Sam swallowed hard. Despite his dad's friendly demeanor, the anxiety he always felt around the man was increasing. "The addition to the cabin is amazing. We hung all the Sheetrock in the bedroom and the bathroom."

Trent nodded. "That's good. The guys we've hired will do the taping this week. That wasn't a job either Joe or I wanted to take on. You think Joe's right about offering it as a vacation rental?"

Holy shit, he's never asked my opinion before. "Yes, vacation rentals are a big thing right now. This area has so few hotels—it should be very successful." Sam watched the football game for a couple of minutes, then he said, "I have something to tell you. I should have said it on Thursday, but... Norah has moved out of our house."

"Oh, Sam," his mother exclaimed.

Sam relayed the entire story, adding, "I'm going to make some changes, starting with coming here more often. I want to ski this winter, and I want to teach Piper. And I'm also going to come up to work on the cabin with Joe."

"You're always welcome here, and we'd love to spend time with Piper. We don't see her nearly enough." Laura looked toward Trent, and he nodded in agreement.

Sam stayed until the end of the game, chatting with his parents in a way he hadn't for years. Trent discussed the flooring options for the cabin with him, and his mother was full of questions about what kinds of toys Piper liked. "Anything having to do with animals," he said. "She's obsessed with animals. No dolls—she doesn't play with them."

When Sam rose to leave, his mom embraced him.

Then Trent stood and reached for Sam's hand. "I'm sorry you're going through this, but you'll be okay."

On the drive home, Sam realized that Matt and Joe weren't exaggerating. This version of Trent did not match his memories. In the past, Trent would have derided him for not being able to maintain the relationship or would have said that Sam should have known better than to get involved with Norah.

Sam rubbed his eyes. He needed to rethink some of his long-held beliefs.

His phone pinged with a text from Joe.

Joe: How'd it go with Mom and Dad?

Sam: It went well, but tell me, where have you hidden the real dad?

Joe: Lol

Sam: Seriously, he asked my opinion about the vacation rental idea. He's never asked my opinion.

Joe: I know, there's a lot that's changed since we moved out.

Sam: I've been gone for over ten years, and he was still busting my chops whenever I talked to him.

Joe: How long since you talked to him? Like, really talked?

Sam: Point taken. Thanks for the weekend.

Chapter Eleven

A Furniture Delivery

SAM SANG ALONG WITH the radio as he drove home from Jesse's the week after Thanksgiving. Dinner had been fun, and after their kids had again clamored for Sam to bring Piper the next time, Jesse and Caitlin had suggested they all visit Sam's house on Saturday afternoon.

He made the turn into his drive, surprised to see lights on at his place. *What the hell? Has Norah come back?* His heart jumped, and his stomach twisted—then he noticed Joe's truck. *Damn. Am I sad or relieved?*

As Sam walked in the door, he came face-to-face with Joe and raised his arms in surprise. "How the fuck did you get into my house?"

"It took me a few minutes, but I found your hidden key." Joe smirked. "The place looks a lot different from when I was here after you guys bought it. You did a fantastic job on the remodel."

Sam shook his head, trying to clear his thoughts. "Thanks. But what are you doing..." He glanced into the dining room, which looked different than it had when he'd left for Jesse's. "Is that table from Mom and Dad's? The one they had when we were kids?"

Joe nodded. "Yup."

"I thought you were tied up in Boston until Christmas." Sam laughed and shook his head again. "What the hell is going on?"

"My *weekends* are busy. I had today off, so I drove up to check on how the walls came out. About the table, well, the official story is that Mom and Dad had furniture stored in the barn, and when you told them Norah took everything, it gave them an excuse to get rid of stuff. Dad asked me to drop it off on my way home."

Sam scratched his head. "Is there an unofficial story?"

"Yeah, the truth." Joe snickered. "They hated the idea of you with no furniture. There's more." He started walking toward the bedrooms, waving his hand to have Sam follow him.

When Joe stopped at the door to Piper's bedroom, Sam peered in. "My God, the bunk bed we had. I can't believe they kept that all this time."

Sam's boyhood bureau sat nestled in a corner of the room. He walked over to it and ran his hand over the top, letting his fingers linger over the *SC* crudely carved in a corner. He barked out a chuckle. "Remember how pissed Mom was when she found out we'd all scratched our initials in our bureaus?"

"Shit, yeah! She grounded us for a month, as I recollect. I missed my first middle school dance." Joe laughed. "The old barn is full of stuff. I don't think they've ever thrown anything away." Joe continued toward Sam's room, where there was a queen-sized bed, another bureau, and nightstands. "I'll help you get the sheets on before I head out. I hate changing the bed by myself. It's one of the worst of many unexpected consequences of my divorce." He sighed ruefully.

Sam looked around in stunned silence for several seconds. "I don't have sheets that size."

"No problem. Mom bought some for this bed and for the bunks too. God, those are going to be a pain in the ass to get on."

Sam joined Joe at the bed and grasped a corner of the sheet Joe tossed at him. He started to pull it over the mattress then looked up quizzically. "This mattress is brand-new."

"Yeah, the mattresses didn't fare too well in that damp old barn." Joe tucked the fitted sheet over the corner. "Plus, would you want to sleep on the mattress that Mom and Dad slept on? And who knows what else?" He leered at Sam before bursting into laughter.

Sam rolled his eyes. "Thanks a lot. I don't need that picture in my head."

They finished Sam's bed and moved to Piper's room. "Pip's been begging for a bunk bed, but Norah wouldn't even consider it. I think changing the sheets was part of it, plus worrying about Pip falling off the bed."

Joe nodded. "She got that right."

"The sheets have puppies!" Sam smiled at the finished result. "Piper's going to lose her mind—a bunk bed and puppies! She's nuts about animals."

"There's still another bed in the barn if you want it for that empty room."

"I might. Quinn mentioned that people at the hospital are always looking for housing. I want to build up my savings. I'm probably going to have to buy out Norah's share of the house."

"Not a bad idea." Joe nodded. "I need to hit the road. It'll take me about two hours to get back to Boston."

Sam felt a little bummed to think of Joe leaving. It felt good having his brother in his house. "Can you stay for a beer?"

Joe hesitated for a few seconds. "Do you have soda? I'm beat, and a beer won't make that drive any easier."

Sam opened the refrigerator. "I've got soda." He pulled one out and handed it to Joe. He reached back in, and his hand hovered over the six-pack before moving back to the cans of soda. "Let's sit in the living room."

Joe sank into the recliner. "Mom said they've never been here."

Sam sat on the couch and leaned forward, elbows on his knees. "Nope. Think they'd like it?"

"Of course." Joe stretched his legs in front of him. "A shrink would have a field day with how we're still looking for Trent Carpenter's approval."

"You too?"

"Oh yeah."

Sam sighed. "So, this was all Mom's idea, right? The furniture, the mattresses, the sheets?"

Joe's mouth quirked into a smile. "I'm pretty sure Dad was on the same page with her about it."

"Talk to me about Dad. Because the man who busted my chops every chance he got would *never* have done this."

"Well, Mom left him shortly after my wedding, for a start."

Sam's eyes went wide. Joe had gotten married five years earlier, and Sam had skipped the ceremony. *What did I miss?* "Did he get drunk?" he asked. "I remember what an ass he made of himself at Matt and Jilly's wedding." Matt had gotten married shortly before Sam started dating Norah. "That was part of the reason I didn't come to yours. I'm sorry about that. It was a dick move."

"Doesn't seem too important now that you didn't make it to the wedding for a marriage that barely lasted four years." Joe shrugged. "I remember that tremendous blowup you and Dad had right after Piper was born because you weren't marrying Norah."

"Yeah. What he couldn't understand was that the choice wasn't mine." Sam grimaced. "Same as you—doesn't seem too important for a relationship that didn't last."

"The atmosphere at my wedding differed from Matt and Jilly's. Instead of a barn in the Vermont hills, we were at a swanky hotel in the city because that's what Tina and her mother wanted." Joe's eyes hardened. "I'll never do that again." He shook his head. "Mom was afraid Dad would go off the deep end. She shared that with me at the rehearsal dinner."

Disgust bubbled up in Sam. "Nice," he said, knowing Joe would recognize his sarcasm.

"Yeah. A couple of weeks later, Mom took stock. Piper was a year old, and she'd only seen her once." Joe studied his can of soda then looked back at Sam, who was watching him intently. "Think about it. She'd raised us three cowboys—imagine how thrilled she was to have a granddaughter to do girly things with. But Mom never saw her."

"If you're trying to make me feel guilty, you're succeeding."

"I'm not. Just trying to show you where her head was." Joe shrugged. "I had almost as little contact with them as you, and even Matt had distanced himself. He transferred to a different part of the factory so he wouldn't have to see Dad on a daily basis. Mom realized it all came down to Dad and the way he treated all of us."

Sam's emotions were mixed. He'd never seen any sign from his mother that his father's behavior bothered her. *Except for that one time after I started dating Quinn, when Dad wanted to throw me out, but he said Mom wouldn't let him.* He was relieved to learn she'd finally seen the truth about her husband but still felt conflicted over the pain he'd caused by staying away. "So, Mom left?"

Joe nodded. "Packed her stuff and moved in with Aunt Michelle. Told Dad she wouldn't be back while he was drinking so heavily and that he needed to learn to control the dark moods."

"How long was she gone?"

"Almost a year."

"Damn." Sam's eyebrows rose in surprise. "I must have talked to her during that time. She calls every couple of months, but she didn't tell me anything. Did you know?"

"Nope. Pretty sad. Neither of us saw her at all during their separation, and Matt knew but didn't tell us. We put the 'dys' in dysfunctional."

Sam took a deep breath and blew it out. "That's putting it mildly. Are you sure you don't want a beer?"

Joe shot a wry smile at Sam and shook his head.

"What made her go back?" Sam asked. "Did Dad go to rehab or join AA?"

"Can you picture Trent Carpenter in rehab?" The corner of Joe's mouth quirked again. "Or at an AA meeting? No, he quit cold turkey. With many backslides along the way. It took several months before he finally stopped altogether." Joe stretched his legs in front of him. "I didn't expect to go into all of this tonight."

"He's going to be mad that you told me."

"No. He said I could tell you if the time seemed right. Matt and I thought about telling you at Thanksgiving, but we wanted to make sure everything was okay with Mom and Dad." Joe yawned. "How about if I sleep on that bottom bunk tonight? I can leave early in the morning."

Sam walked to the kitchen and came back with two bottles of beer. "If you're staying, you can have a drink."

Joe laughed as he twisted the cap off. "Have Dad tell you about quitting sometime. He puts a funny spin on it." Joe took a long swallow from the bottle. "After he finally got clean, he realized he felt like shit physically, and the dark moods were still there. He tried to muscle through but finally listened to Mom and sought medical help."

"So they stayed in touch while Mom was at Aunt Michelle's?"

"Oh yeah, he was begging her to come back. And Mom always loved him, but she told him she wouldn't live like that anymore."

"It must have killed him to go to a doctor. Remember how he was about hospitals and doctors?"

"It probably saved his life. The doctor diagnosed him with depression and prescribed meds for it. He'll tell you—he was in a deep hole after he gave up alcohol while he was living without Mom."

"How did she decide to go back?"

"She went to some of his counseling sessions—"

"Holy shit," Sam interrupted before he sprawled back on the couch. "Counseling? He *has* changed."

Joe took another swallow of his beer. "He was at rock-bottom, knowing he'd lost us and unsure if Mom would come back or not. He had no choice."

Sam rubbed his jaw. "The only time I saw Mom and Dad after Piper was born was when Gram or Aunt Michelle had something going on." He raised the beer bottle to his lips. "Maybe that's why I didn't know about the separation. And I always made it a point to stay far away from Dad at those gatherings. Was it like that for you too?"

Joe nodded. "Pretty much."

"When did you start going up there again?"

"The guys at the shop who worked with Dad were telling Matt how much easier he was to get along with, so Matt started dropping in at their house. He let me know what was going on. Then two years ago, Dad reached out and asked me to come up. The change was obvious." Joe scratched the back of his neck and narrowed his eyes at Sam. "You had to have noticed it right away at Thanksgiving."

Sam tented his hands in front of his face, thinking before he answered. "I did, but I figured he was on his best behavior for the holiday. When I returned on Sunday, that's when it hit home." He paused. "I must admit, I've still been skeptical. Until tonight. You showing up with the furniture and telling me all this makes me think... maybe it's for real."

"It's for real. He'll tell you it's a constant battle but one he's determined to win." Joe stood. "Five o'clock is going to come too soon. I need to go to bed. Are you going to sleep on the top bunk, like old times?" He grinned at Sam.

On Friday night, Norah pulled up to drop off Piper, and Sam clenched his teeth as he watched them getting out of the car. He'd had to work late, so Norah picked up Piper and was dropping her off for the weekend. He glanced around then hurried to the kitchen to move the dirty dishes from the counter to the dishwasher.

Piper burst through the door. "D-D-Daddy!"

Joy rushed through Sam as she ran into his arms, and he lifted her into the air. "Piper!"

Her eyes traveled to the dining room. "You got a t-t-table! Where did that come from?"

"From your grandparents." He set her back on the floor.

"From Nana and Pop?" Piper asked, referring to Norah's parents.

"No, it came from *my* parents." The confused look on Piper's face appalled him all over again. "Go look in your bedroom."

As Piper scooted down the hallway, Norah eyed Sam. "Your parents brought you furniture? They've never even been here, unless they've come since I've been gone."

"Actually, my brother Joe delivered it for them..."

"B-b-bunk beds!" Piper's delighted squeal filled the hallway, making Sam grin. "Mommy, D-D-Daddy, come see!"

Norah placed her hand on Sam's arm, holding him back as he started toward Piper's bedroom. "Bunk beds? Do you think that's a good idea? What if she falls off?"

"Joe, Matt, and I all slept in them, and we survived." He looked at her with irritation. "God, Norah, there's a safety rail. She's excited—don't spoil that."

They walked down the hall, and he remembered walking through the house with Norah in happier times. Going together to tuck Piper in at night or heading to their bedroom for a night of passion. He shook his head to dispel the images.

"Look, the sheets have p-p-puppies! Can I sleep on the t-t-top?"

"You can try it." Sam nodded. "As long as you promise not to fall off." He winked at her.

Norah looked on in silence as Piper ran to Sam's room and exclaimed over the bed in there. When she returned to Sam and Norah, she asked, "May I watch TV before d-d-dinner?"

Sam nodded, and Piper hugged Norah before running to the living room.

Norah turned to leave. "That was a gracious gesture from your parents."

Is she trying to make conversation? "Yeah, it was." *This is even more awkward than talking to Quinn for the first time after ten years.*

Norah paused by the kitchen island. "We have a meeting with a mediator on Tuesday." She reached into her purse and pulled out a business card, which she held out for Sam to take, but his arms remained at his sides. She laid it on the island.

Sam took a step back, his emotions in turmoil as he looked at the card on the counter. "Do you genuinely think that's necessary?"

"We need to decide on some things. Like what we're going to do with the house and if we want to continue with the way Piper is splitting her time between us." At least Norah's voice was soft this time, nothing like the ice-filled tone she had used when she told him she was leaving.

"Can't we figure that out on our own?" Sam took a deep breath. "Do we need to involve a third party?"

"It's been over a month, Sam. You've barely said two words to me, and your anger is obvious. What makes you think we'll be able to have a civil discussion? A neutral mediator will make it easier." She glanced toward Piper. "I don't want to fight anymore."

Sam rubbed his jaw. "I guess I don't have a choice. I'll be there." He turned toward the refrigerator. "Now, if you don't mind, I need to start dinner for Pip and me."

SLMMER OF RAIN

Chapter Twelve
The Mediator Post Mortem

SAM PUSHED OPEN THE door to the Sidecar, a pub in downtown White River. The crowd was thin, not surprising on a Tuesday night, and he found a table, ordered a beer, then leaned back in his chair, closing his eyes momentarily.

He'd dreaded the meeting with the mediator, and while it hadn't been as bad as he expected, the experience had drained him. Between the counseling and working with the speech-language pathologist on Piper's stutter, he and Norah had already brought plenty of outside people into their relationship. Laying everything out in front of yet another person had been rough.

Norah pushed for an every-other-day custody arrangement, citing the difficulty of going five days without seeing Piper. Sam knew that would be challenging for him with the commitments he had on Wednesday and Thursday. He didn't want to give up dinner at Jesse's, and on Thursday nights, he often needed to attend municipal commission meetings for the projects he was working on.

When it came to the house, Norah agreed to pay half the mortgage until June, then he would need to refinance and buy out her share or sell the house. During their discussion of the holidays, she asked him to stay with her and Piper on Christmas Eve so that they would be together on Christmas morning. Norah was being generous, he knew, but he still could not get past his anger. He'd been unable to address her directly and could barely look at her.

Thank God Piper is spending the night with Norah's sister, Betsy. I need this time to decompress. Even though Sam understood how much Piper loved her Aunt Betsy, he'd been hesitant to let her stay there—it meant missing out on part of his time with Pip. When Norah suggested it, he'd briefly wondered if Norah had given up any of *her* time to Betsy.

Stop. Just stop. He had to remind himself constantly that Piper was not a pawn on a chessboard or a prize to be fought over.

Sam drank three beers in quick succession as he stewed over the mediation. He ordered another one as his mind drifted to Quinn and how he longed to see her. Would she come if he called? He'd been half hoping to run into her shopping in Lebanon, but that hadn't happened.

After a hazy internal debate, he picked up his phone and punched in her number.

"Sam?"

His heart jumped at the sound of her voice. "Hey, Quinn. I could use a friend to talk to." He heard himself slur the words and hoped she wouldn't notice.

"Have you been drinking?"

"Why, yes. Yes, I have been, or rather, I am. I think I'm near you. That's why I called. And because you're my friend. You are my friend, right?"

"Where are you?"

Damn. He'd hoped she would reassure him on the friend front. "I'm at the Sidecar."

"I can be there in about fifteen minutes. Don't go anywhere."

Quinn was coming. He was going to see her after a month of missing her all over again.

He saw her enter the bar. Her dark, wavy hair cascaded over her shoulders, while leggings and a blue sweater accentuated her curves. His cock jumped to attention at the sight of her. This was why he hadn't wanted to go beyond kissing with Becca. He only wanted Quinn.

She frowned at him as she walked over. "After we drank so much in Boston that night, didn't you swear off drinking like that ever again?" She pulled out a chair and joined him at the table. "Looks like you didn't even last six weeks."

"I didn't last long at all after you bowed out of my life," he said. "You could say I am not adjusting well to being alone. I have consumed copious amounts of alcohol." *Why does she care about my drinking? I have it under control. I don't drink when I have Piper. It's only when I'm alone.*

Quinn's brown eyes didn't hold the same warmth that he remembered. She placed one hand on the table. Sam reached out to caress it, but Quinn pulled her arm away, tucking it into her lap.

"So, what's going on tonight that made you call me?" she asked. "I thought I made it clear we shouldn't stay in touch, at least for a while. And why are you in White River?"

"Norah and I went to mediation today. Did you know that at the end of a relationship, you get to go to mediation? It's great fun." Sam caught the server's eye and signaled for another beer. "The mediator's office is near here. At the end, the only thing I wanted was a drink. Actually, several drinks. And then I thought about you." He accepted his new beer and took a long swallow. "So, I called."

When she didn't respond, his heart sank. Still, he said, "I didn't think you'd come."

"You said you needed a friend to talk to, and you sounded drunk. I'm concerned for your safety."

"Concerned for my safety? How formal." He snorted. "I *am* drunk and need a friend to talk to. I hated listening to Norah outline why her plan for sharing Piper was better than mine. And learning that I might have to sell the house to meet my financial obligations. My financial obligations!" He drained his glass and slammed it down.

"I thought you were trying to avoid getting angry like this."

"Hell yes, I'm angry." He took a breath, trying to get back under control. "I don't want any of this. Piper shuttling back and forth between us, not getting to see her at Thanksgiving, selling the house I put so much time into. It all sucks." He began gesturing to the server to bring another beer.

Quinn placed her hand over his and said, "You should stop."

He shrugged off her hand and considered ordering the beer anyway, but instead he put his head down, and when he looked up, he averted his gaze from Quinn.

"I've been a prick to Norah. She drops Piper off, and I don't say a word to her." He swallowed the suddenly bitter taste in his mouth. "She's being generous with me, paying her part of the mortgage, at least, for a while, and inviting me to stay at her place on Christmas Eve so we'll both be there with Piper on Christmas morning." He brought his eyes back to Quinn. "She looked so sad this afternoon. But the anger comes over me in waves."

Quinn held his gaze but didn't offer any thoughts on what he said about Norah. "You shouldn't drive home. You can stay in my guest room."

His house was twenty miles away on a winding dirt road, so Quinn was right. But was there more to her taking him home?

She left the table to talk to the bartender. When she returned, she said, "Let's go. Your car will be okay here until morning."

As they walked to Quinn's car, he slid his arm over her shoulder, trying to draw her closer. "Your guest room? Don't you mean your bed?"

Quinn stepped to the side, out of his reach. "I said guest room, and that's what I meant."

When they arrived at her townhouse, Quinn led him to the kitchen. "Sit. I'm going to make you something to eat."

Sam watched as she pulled out her phone and sent a text. He knew she'd gotten a reply when she smiled, put the phone on the counter, and started scrambling some eggs. "Who are you texting at this hour?"

She slid a plate in front of him but didn't answer his question. Sam ate the food and then pushed the plate away. He gazed at Quinn where she sat across from him then reached over and rested his hand lightly on her arm. "I miss you. Remember how good it was being together in Boston? I'm thinking about it all the time. Want to taste you again, want to make you moan, want to be inside you again. Do you think about it?"

"No." Quinn's reply, punctuated by her arm sliding out of his grasp, took all the wind from his sails. She pushed back from the table. "I'm going to clean up, and then I'll show you the guest room. You need to sleep off the alcohol."

Sam wandered into the living room, where Quinn's hiking pictures caught his interest. The only peak he recognized was Mount Pisgah, which was near his hometown. He tried to get closer to one of the photos, but there was a bookcase blocking the way. Finally, he took the photo off the wall to get a good look, then he walked back to the kitchen, carrying the picture. "Is this the doctor we met in Boston?"

Quinn's eyes looked furious as she reached for the picture. "What the hell are you doing? You had no business taking that off the wall!"

Sam backed away. "How'd you get..." Before he could finish, he tripped over his unsteady feet and fumbled the frame before it crashed to the floor, shattering the glass. "Shit! I'm sorry." He bent to pick it up. "I didn't mean—"

"Shut up!" Quinn pushed him away. "I don't care what you meant!"

Sam watched as she picked up the frame carefully before placing it on the table. He could not wrap his mind around it, that Quinn and the doctor were... what, dating? Already?

Still, it didn't excuse what he'd done. Ashamed, he stood helplessly to the side as Quinn swept up the glass.

When she finished, she looked at him, still clearly pissed. "You're nothing but a drunk! I should take you back to the Sidecar and dump you." She took a deep breath, visibly trembling with the force of her anger. "But I don't want to be responsible if you have an accident and kill yourself. Or worse yet, someone else."

Her words cut him deeply, and Sam staggered back, raising his hands to cover his face. "God, Quinn, I'm sorry..."

"Save it," she snarled.

She led him to the guest room and, as she closed the door, Sam tried to apologize again. "I'm so sorry—"

"Go to sleep, Sam," she barked. "I'm not interested in your hollow apology."

Sam undressed and crawled under the covers. *Man, what the hell is wrong with me? I'm such a fuckup...*

When he woke up, his first thought was of how he'd dropped the picture and incurred Quinn's wrath. What was it going to be like facing her? He got up clumsily.

There was a rap on his door, then her curt voice announced, "I'll make you some breakfast. We need to leave in half an hour."

Feeling nauseous, Sam righted himself and slunk into the kitchen, where he sat down opposite her in front of a plate of peanut-butter toast, coffee, and some Tylenol.

He made himself look at her. "I was obnoxious and out of line last night. I'm sorry."

"Yeah, you were," Quinn said. "But I shouldn't have called you a drunk."

Sam shrugged and began to eat. "The shoe fit last night. I need to get myself together."

The picture he'd broken sat at the end of the table, almost like a third person. He couldn't keep from looking at it. "Can I ask you about that?"

"His sister lives in Hanover, and we've been seeing each other when he comes to visit her. We went hiking."

"Is that the real reason you broke it off with me?"

Quinn shook her head. "No. I didn't hear from him until after you and I were done."

"*You* were done. I'm not sure I was." Sam forced a smile. "Is it serious?"

The happiness that spread across her face was almost blinding. "I'm falling in love with him."

Sam's heart sank. "I really have lost you, haven't I?"

"I wasn't yours to lose, Sam."

He sighed. "I know, I know. I'm happy for you." *Should be. Will be. Eventually.* "I didn't like the idea of you being alone." He drained his coffee mug. "I really miss you, though—not only the sex but talking to you. The week in Boston felt like it did when we first met. I know you were right about me not being ready to move on. But could we stay in touch, maybe by text?"

He would take whatever crumbs he could get if it meant keeping her in his life.

Quinn started loading the dishwasher. "I don't know, Sam." Her hesitation came through loud and clear.

"I know how needy this sounds, but the only other person I have to talk to is Jesse, and he's probably tired of listening to me whine." He supposed that wasn't strictly true, now that he'd reconnected with Joe, but he still wasn't sure if this happy-family business was going to last.

"You think I want to listen to you?" Quinn asked as she pulled her hair into a ponytail like he'd seen her do so many times before. "I can't be texting with you all the time."

"I get it. But once in a while, if I need a friend to talk to?" He tried out a grin and found it felt okay. "I'll keep the whining to a minimum, I promise."

"Fine, but don't push it."

As they were driving back to the Sidecar, his phone pinged.

> Norah: *Can we meet, just you and me? I realize I started this, but I don't like how things are. I miss us.*

"Son of a bitch," he muttered.

"What?" Quinn asked.

He sighed. "Norah just texted me. She wants to meet, misses me." Sam looked at Quinn. "Do you think this means there's a chance to work things out? Do I even want to do that?"

Quinn shook her head. "That's on you."

Once they reached his car, Sam climbed out of hers, and Quinn leaned over. "Sam, I hope you find your answers. They aren't at the bottom of a beer bottle."

"I know." He gazed at her, a little sad, a lot grateful. "Thanks for rescuing me. I'll be in touch."

Sam spent the day suffering from a hangover and obsessing over the text from Norah, which made his head hurt even more than the alcohol from the night before. Quinn's words had hit home.

When I see Jesse tonight, I'm going to ask him to recommend a therapist. He has contacts in that world and knows me well enough to pick someone who will be a good fit.

At the end of the day, Sam closed his laptop, picked up his phone, then scrolled to Norah's name in the messaging app. He stared at her name, rubbed his forehead, and inhaled deeply before typing. When he was done, his finger hovered over the send button for several seconds before he stabbed it and exhaled the breath he'd been holding.

Sam: Why don't you come for dinner on Sunday, around five? We can talk after Piper goes to bed.

Within seconds, her response pinged.

Norah: Okay.

Sam walked out of his office wondering what he and Norah would talk about. On his way to Jesse's, he stopped at a store in West Lebanon. He picked out a frame that matched the one he'd dropped the night before and detoured to Quinn's townhouse, where he wrote a message on the bag. *I'm so sorry for my behavior last night. Thanks for being there for me.* He propped the bag against her door and continued his drive to Jesse's house.

Chapter Thirteen

A Visit From Trent

THE NEXT NIGHT, SAM nursed a beer as he remembered telling Jesse about his douchey behavior with Quinn. Jesse didn't pass judgement—he never did—and he said he'd help Sam find a therapist. It would be after the holidays before anyone had openings. Sam hoped it wasn't too long. Now that he'd decided to make changes in his behavior, and realized he couldn't do it on his own, he wanted to move forward.

He had popped the top on a second beer when he heard a vehicle in his driveway. *What the hell?* Beer in hand, he opened the door and recognized his father's truck. As he watched Trent climb out, his stomach clenched as it always had at his father's approach, ever since he was a teenager.

"Dad." Sam hoped his voice didn't disclose his discomfort. "What are you doing here?"

"One of my guys had a serious car accident, and he's in the hospital down here." Trent had been a supervisor at the factory for as long as Sam could remember. "I wanted to check on him. Thought I'd stop by here and see if everything worked out okay with the furniture."

Trent Carpenter, driving an hour and a half to check on a coworker. Sam remembered him as a self-centered son of a bitch. The well-being of coworkers, of anyone really, was not high on his list. *This is just nuts.* Sam opened the door wider. "Come on in. The furniture is great. Thanks again." He had called his mother to express his gratitude the night after Joe's delivery.

As they walked into the kitchen, Sam noticed Trent was holding a to-go coffee cup, and Sam quietly placed his beer on the counter. "Welcome," he said nervously.

"Joe said you remodeled the whole place." His father looked around, taking in the tile floors, dark cabinets, and quartz countertops. "You did a nice job."

"Let me show you the rest." For once, Sam was able to be in his comfort zone with his father, showing off his house and the work he'd done on it. He led Trent into the living room, which had hardwood floors and that enormous stone fireplace dominating the space.

Trent ran his hands over the stones. "You did this?"

Sam nodded.

"It's beautiful." He grinned at Sam. "Looks like you learned something from working on all those fixer-uppers your mom and I bought when you were in high school and college."

Sam smiled back. "I'll admit, there were moments when I said a brief prayer of thanks for all the experience I had."

Trent walked around, looking at the woodwork and returning to the fireplace to study it more closely. After a moment, he said, "I pushed you boys too hard," while still looking at the fireplace.

Sam automatically waved one hand to dismiss his father's words. "We all survived."

"You did." Trent turned toward Sam. "In spite of me. Can we sit?"

"Sure." Sam studied his father as Trent took a drink of his coffee, knowing that in the past, Trent would have added liquor to the cup. *He seems sober, but I'm still waiting for an explosion.* He picked up his phone. "Want to see what it looked like before?"

"Absolutely." Trent reached for Sam's phone.

Sam held his breath as Trent studied the photos, realizing how much he wanted validation from his father.

Trent nodded as he swiped from slide to slide. "Really nice work." He handed the phone back to Sam. "You did a good job. I'm proud of you."

"Thank you." Sam's smile widened, and his stomach clenched in an unfamiliar way. A good way. He'd never heard words like those from his father. "Your opinion means a lot."

Trent nodded, his expression serious. "I know Joe told you about my struggles."

"A little."

"Come on now—he told you the whole sad tale. You can admit it." He paused. "I haven't known how to reach out to you. I'd hoped when Joe started texting you last spring that you'd come up and that would break the ice. Pretty cowardly of me." After finishing his coffee, Trent continued, "I was even harder on you than I was on Joe and Matt. You had bigger dreams than they did. Or at least, you talked about them more." He sighed. "I saw myself in you."

Slowly, Trent stood and walked over to the fireplace, then he turned back to Sam. "Laura and I were already expecting Joe when we got married."

Duh. "Yeah, I figured that out when I was in high school."

Trent scoffed. "Of course you did. When you started dating Quinn, I feared the same thing happening to you. I thought your dreams would go up in smoke, so I gave you shit about dating her and then Ginger. I was sure you'd get trapped into marriage."

"Do you think Mom trapped you?"

"No. I love your mother. I found out how much when she moved out." Trent grimaced. "But back then, I felt trapped by the circumstances. We both did. We would have married eventually, but there were things we would have done first." He walked back to the recliner and sat down. "I love all you boys, and I'm so damn proud of what you've accomplished. Again, in spite of me."

Sam stood. "I'm going to get a soda. Do you want one?" When Trent nodded, Sam walked to the refrigerator, looked longingly at his beer, then grabbed two sodas and returned to the living room.

Trent accepted the can. "Can we start over? We'd like to see you more often. And we'd like to get to know our granddaughter. You mentioned skiing—will you stay with us when you come to the mountain?"

"I've been thinking about that." Sam relaxed into a smile. "Piper's an incredible little kid. You'll love her."

Trent smiled back tentatively. "We've talked about Christmas with Joe and Matt. We know you'll be sharing Piper with Norah. It's okay with us if our celebration can't be on Christmas day. We'd like to be all together."

Sam thought for a minute. *You told Joe you want to make some changes.* "Pip's going to be with me for a few days while she's on vacation, so... we could come up the day after Christmas." He took a deep breath. "And stay overnight, if that works for you and Mom." *That'll give me a chance to see if this is real. If it goes okay for one night, maybe we can do a weekend in January when we go skiing.*

Trent's grin widened. "That will be perfect."

The Saturday after his father's impromptu visit, Sam and Piper dressed in warm outdoor clothes for a trip to a Christmas tree farm. Despite the holiday being a week away, not much snow had fallen, so walking was easy as they moved among the trees, looking for the right one. Sam didn't want one that was too big, since Norah had taken all the decorations.

Sam picked a five-foot-tall tree and began cutting.

As it fell, Piper ran to a small tree a slight distance away. "C-can we get this one for my room?"

Sam cut it down, too, and delighted in Piper's smile, as bright as the star that would sit on top of the tree.

The store at the farm had everything they needed for decorations, so Sam picked out colored lights as well as gold-and-red garland.

"D-D-Daddy, d-don't we want these lights?" Piper held a package containing white lights.

"Mommy will use the white lights. I think something different, more colorful, would be nice for you and me." Sam cocked his head. "Is that okay with you?"

"Janey's tree has colored lights. I *love* them!" She pointed at the garland. "C-can that go on my tree?"

Sam nodded and gathered Piper into a hug.

At home, Piper said, "C-can we string popcorn to go on the t-t-tree?"

"Sorry, baby girl. We don't have the popcorn or the needle and thread to do that." When her face fell, Sam smiled gently.

"But we can do this." He cut brightly colored construction paper into strips and showed Piper how to join them to make a chain. Over the next hour, they fashioned a chain long enough to go on the tree in Piper's room, then they finished decorating both trees.

After they finished, Sam looked around, knowing the state of the house was far below Norah's standards. "Piper, I need you to help me tidy up."

"Why? I d-d-don't want to. It's f-fine."

"No, it's not. You have toys and clothes all over the place, and so do I."

Piper frowned at him.

"Okay, I don't have toys out here, but I have clothes. Stuff needs to be put away. We put that nice bureau and the Christmas tree in your room. Try to make the rest of the space look good." He paused. "Let's set a timer for fifteen minutes and see which of us can do more."

Sam set the timer, and they started. The house looked better when the timer sounded, and he suggested they do another fifteen minutes. When they finished, he was satisfied. The place wasn't as tidy as Norah would keep it, but it wasn't a mess.

"I have a surprise for you," he said. "Mommy is coming for dinner tomorrow night."

Piper jumped up and down. "What are we going to eat? I can show her m-my b-bureau and my tree." When he told her they would have spaghetti and garlic bread, she squealed. "That's m-my favorite!"

Chapter Fourteen

Last Minute Christmas Shopping

Promptly at five on Sunday evening, there was a knock at the door, and Norah walked in. *Is it weird that she walked in here like it's still her home?* Sam rubbed his jaw. *She did knock, so there's that.* His Norah-related turmoil had begun to boil immediately, despite his effort to tamp it down. He wanted to have a civil conversation with her, especially while Piper was with them.

Piper ran into Norah's arms like she hadn't seen her in months. "C-come see my room!" Piper pulled her mother down the hall.

They finally came back to the kitchen as he was putting the food on the table.

"The bureau looks cute," Norah said. "Pip said she helped paint it."

"She did quite a bit. We made a mess. When I called my mom to thank her for the furniture, she suggested I look on Pinterest for ideas to fix it up." When Norah raised her eyebrows, he smiled a genuine smile, surprising himself. "Yeah, not anything I knew I needed."

"How is your mom?"

"She's good. I went there for Thanksgiving and stayed with Joe and Matt at camp the whole weekend." He told her a little about the work being done at the cabin and that Matt and Jilly were expecting a baby.

"That's exciting. Haven't they had some trouble in that area?"

"Yes, but she's pretty far along now, and everything is fine so far."

When they finished eating, Norah offered to do the dishes.

"No, I'll take care of them," Sam said. "Why don't you go into the living room, and Piper can read to you? Then we can all play a game before her bedtime. She had a shower this morning."

Sam finished the dishes and stood in the dining room, listening to Piper read to Norah. Their daughter's reading was at an advanced level, but the stutter slowed her down. He entered the living room as she finished the book. Piper smoked them both in a game of Candy Land before Sam sent her to get into her pajamas.

"It's a pretty tree," Norah commented.

"Thanks. We went to a tree farm yesterday. I thought the colored lights would be a pleasant change."

They both tucked Piper in and returned to the living room. Sam went to the kitchen for a beer and brought Norah a glass of wine. She was sitting on the couch, so he sat in the recliner facing her.

"I thought the mediation went well."

Oh yeah. So well that I drank myself almost to oblivion and made an unwelcome advance on Quinn. He looked toward the Christmas tree. "Do you think that if we spend time together like this on the weekends, what we've been doing could work? I could come to your place for pizza on Friday nights when you have her, and you could come here on Sunday. Then we'd only go a couple of days without seeing her. With my schedule, Monday and Tuesday work the best for me to have her."

Norah thought for a minute. "That's a good plan. The mediator is there to make recommendations. We can do what we want. But we need to agree. You'll stay Christmas Eve?"

"Yeah, it'll be good for her. I'm giving her skis for Christmas."

Norah's eyes widened. "You *are*?"

"Yes. I'm going to ski this winter, and I want her to learn. Pip and I talked about it."

"I wish you would have talked to me about it." Norah's voice was halfway to the icy tone she'd used right after she moved out.

"I grew up skiing with my family, Norah. It's something I want to do with my daughter. I'm sorry that you never wanted to try it."

Her jaw tightened a little. "Are you going to take her skiing during Christmas vacation? And where will you go?"

"I'm going to take her to Burke—it's familiar and an easy drive. We won't start until January. Vacation's too busy. But Pip and I are going up to my parent's house on the day after Christmas and staying overnight."

"You haven't done that in the whole time I've known you."

"No, I haven't. And not for years, even before we met." He sighed. "My dad's made some big changes. I'm a little nervous that it's a temporary thing, but Joe and Matt both told me he acts very differently from how he used to. And the changes happened a year or two ago. It's not like it just started, but time will tell."

"You'll leave if things get bad?" Norah asked. "I don't want Piper around the behavior you've described to me."

Sam took a deep breath. "Norah, can't you give me a little credit? I don't want her to see his black moods either." He tried to keep his tone even. "Alcohol played a big role in those moods, and my dad's completely stopped drinking. But if I see any sign of his temper getting out of control, we'll leave."

When Norah didn't respond after a long pause, Sam tamped down his rising temper and said, "I love Piper as much as you do, and I know how to take care of her."

Norah nodded. "I know." She cleared her throat. "Can we talk about Christmas Eve? I bought us Christmas pajamas." That tradition started when Piper was a baby, so no surprise that Norah was keeping it going.

"Piper loves that. She bought you a present when we went shopping."

Norah smiled. "She has a present for you as well. I bought the stuff for her stocking, but I wasn't sure about you and me doing stockings for each other."

Sam thought for a minute. "We need to do them. She still believes in Santa. It would be weird if there weren't stockings for us when we've had them in the past." He shrugged. "It might not be as elaborate as in other years, but I'll do something."

"I agree." A little hesitantly, she reached her hand across the distance between them and placed it on top of Sam's. "You don't seem as angry with me as you were."

He wished it were truer. "I'm working through it. Piper doesn't see that anger—I make sure of it. And I don't say anything negative about you." He left his hand under hers.

"The stutter's not getting any better."

Sam shook his head. "There's a lot going on with the holidays. Let's see how she's doing when life calms down."

"Okay." Norah studied him. "I'm surprised at you recognizing the stress the holidays bring. You always seemed oblivious in the past."

Sam shrugged. "Oh, I recognized it, but... I don't know. My reaction differs from yours."

"I should get going." Norah stood.

Sam said nothing, just nodded. Once she was gone, he shut the door behind her and clenched his fists. *Dammit. She's never going to consider me her equal in the parenting department.* He opened another beer. Based on what Norah had said, he'd been able to keep his anger from being obvious, but he'd still been seething inside at her reaction to the idea of Piper skiing and staying with his parents.

He leaned his head back and closed his eyes. Between the interaction with Norah and him only needing one beer to decompress, the night counted as a win.

Three days later, Sam checked out of work early to shop for Norah's stocking, wishing he had thought of it sooner. He wasn't looking forward to being caught up in the crush of last-minute shoppers.

Sam found several items he knew Norah would like and was almost ready to check out when the store's jewelry selection caught his eye. He picked up and discarded several bracelets before finally settling on one that he added to the pile of items in his handcart. Looking up, he noticed an auburn-haired woman. She looked familiar, and when she raised her hand in a wave, he remembered where he'd seen her before.

"Sophie." His eyebrows raised. "Did I get that right?"

"Yes. Last-minute shopping?" She followed him to the checkout, where several people were ahead of them, waiting to pay.

Sam grimaced. "Something like that. You too?" He looked at the necklace in her hand.

"Actually, I'm buying for myself." She tittered, looking and sounding self-conscious. "I get what I want that way."

"Not a bad plan." Sam smiled. They moved forward a few inches as the people in front of them completed their purchases. "I've never shopped this late. And I'll never do it again."

Sophie nodded. "Will you—" She stopped herself.

Sam peered at her. "Will I what?"

"I don't mean to pry." Sophie's face flushed. "I was going to ask... will you be with your daughter? I know you were upset at Thanksgiving, about not having her with you." She paused. "It's none of my business."

"We're spending the holiday together." He inhaled deeply and blew it out. "The three of us."

Sophie smiled. "You reconciled! That's great."

They edged closer to the cash register.

Sam frowned and struggled to keep his voice even when he said, "No."

"Oh God," Sophie groaned. "I'm sorry. I shouldn't have jumped to that conclusion. I'll shut up now."

Sam paid for his items and stood at the end of the counter, juggling his two bags, while Sophie paid for her necklace. Once she was done, he looked at her. "Sorry for barking at you like that. I'm going to grab a coffee at Cara's. Would you like to join me?"

Sophie hesitated before saying, "Uh, sure."

They walked silently to Cara's Coffee Shop, and as soon as they were in the door, Sam nudged her, pointing toward the corner. "Go grab that table while I order. What do you want?"

"I... I can get my own."

"There's no time for discussion." Sam grinned, hoping she was feeling conspiratorial. "We need that table!" He looked at her expectantly. "Your order?"

She laughed a little. "Peppermint mocha, medium, and a chocolate donut." With a nod, she moved toward the table.

Sam nudged her again. "Hurry!"

Sam watched her slide into the booth, barely beating out a couple of teenage girls, and he flashed her a thumbs-up as he waited in the long line. Sophie smiled, making him feel better than he had all afternoon.

Once he had their order, Sam placed the tray on the table and slipped off his jacket before sitting down. "This place is nuts."

He took a bite of his maple-frosted donut and washed it down with a swallow of coffee then sighed and pointed to the donut. "Only one of these would get me to fight this crowd."

Sophie moaned softly after taking a bite of her donut. "I know. I spend far too much time here. Sorry I pried into your personal business back there." Sophie waved her hand in the store's direction.

He nodded. "Norah invited me to stay on Christmas Eve. You know, so we'll both be with Piper on Christmas morning." It all came out in a rush. "But we're not reconciling."

"Again, sorry for making assumptions."

"Don't worry about it." Sam managed a small smile. "I was shopping for Norah's stocking. Santa can't leave anyone out. I didn't even think about it until she invited me to stay overnight." He paused. "I'm... still adjusting to the separation."

She gazed at him sympathetically. "It must be hard."

"Yeah." He nodded. *Time to change the subject.* "So, you had all your shopping done... except for yourself?"

"Something like that."

Sam leaned back in the booth. "Well, I can tell you I'm glad to be finished." He looked at Sophie over the top of his coffee cup. "How's it going at the school?"

"Quite well." She smiled. "It's much smaller than other schools I've worked at. I enjoy being able to connect with the students more deeply."

"Pip loves all her teachers," Sam said then rolled his eyes. "I hope that lasts."

Sophie studied him for a minute. "You really do her pigtails?"

"What?" Sam laughed. "You think real men can't braid?"

"Well…"

"Even before Norah moved out, I was in charge of mornings, and I taught myself how to do Pip's hair. I do a mean French braid too. When you see her on Tuesday or Wednesday, that's my artwork. And sometimes on Monday too." Sam knew he was bragging, but both he and Sophie were smiling.

"She's lucky to have you."

"No. I'm the lucky one. She's the best thing in my life." Sam ate the last bite of his donut. "Are you headed home for Christmas?"

"No." Sophie hesitated. "It's too far."

"Where are you from?"

Sophie rubbed her finger around the rim of her cup. "I grew up in Rhode Island, but I don't have anyone left there. I'm looking forward to relaxing during the break." She held up and rattled a bag from the bookstore. "I have reading to catch up on."

"Sounds a little lonely."

Sophie paused before she answered. "Not really. The staff at the school has been exceptionally welcoming. I work out almost every night, and despite the short time I've been here, I've made a couple of good friends at the gym. Maybe you know them—Ali White and Brenda Young? I've found everybody seems to know everybody else here." She grinned.

"That's small-town life for you." Sam smiled back at her. "Ali is married to Chad White, isn't she? He's a real estate developer. My company has worked on a couple of projects with him."

Sophie nodded, and after swallowing the rest of her coffee, she reached for her wallet. "My order usually costs something like this." She slid six dollars toward Sam.

"Don't be ridiculous. It's my treat."

Sophie protested, but Sam pushed the money back toward her, then he stood.

"I need to head home," he said. "I hope you have a Merry Christmas, Sophie."

"You too."

Sam followed her back to the parking lot and watched Sophie drop the bills she'd tried to give him into the kettle of a bell-ringing Santa. *Nice. I wonder if she wears that green coat because it matches her eyes? I didn't notice them that day at the school, but I was mesmerized today.*

He chuckled a little. *"Mesmerized," good God. When was the last time I thought of a woman's eyes that way?* He shook his head at himself and waved to Sophie as she drove away.

Chapter Fifteen

Christmas Celebrations

SAM BRAVED THE CROWDS again on Christmas Eve to stop at Cara's for donuts. Christmas breakfast had included Cara's since he and Norah moved into the house.

While he stood in line, he realized Norah hadn't even crossed his mind when he was at the coffee shop the day before. Sharing a coffee with Sophie had been a pleasant diversion. *Too bad she's spending the holiday all alone.*

A light snow was falling as Sam drove to Norah's house. The skis, boots, and helmet for Piper were in his back seat. Wrapping the skis had been a struggle, but he knew she wouldn't care about how the package looked.

Sam was happy to see more snow. After a big storm the weekend before, the ten-day forecast was for continued cold weather.

They had plans to ski on the second weekend in January, and if the weather held, the conditions should be perfect.

Sam had been to Norah's house twice right after he returned from Boston because Piper was having difficulty adjusting. There had been boxes everywhere, but Sam noticed the house was significantly smaller than the one they'd shared, which surprised him. He was about to knock when the door opened.

Piper jumped into his arms. "D-Daddy, Daddy! Santa is c-coming t-tonight!"

"I know! Are you all ready for him?"

"Yes! We b-baked cookies, and we b-bought carrots for his reindeer."

He grinned. "It sounds like you've covered all the bases." Her excitement was contagious, making him the most relaxed he had been around Norah since she moved out.

"Mommy, can I give D-Daddy the tour?"

He'd only seen the living room on his previous visits. Norah nodded and kept putting the finishing touches on dinner as Piper showed him around.

"This is M-M-Mommy's room, this is the office, and here's my room." The walls were lavender and dark purple, with white curtains and a multicolored comforter. Her books filled a small bookcase, and her stuffed animals decorated the bed.

Piper led him back to the living room. "See our new c-couch and chairs? A ch-chair for each of us." The living room had a love seat and two recliners. Sam wondered where Norah intended for him to sleep—the love seat must fold out into a bed.

After dinner, they each opened a present.

"Christmas pajamas!" Piper exclaimed. "We have to put them on!"

Norah went to change in her room while Sam went into the bathroom, and when they all came back together, Piper insisted they take a picture.

One big happy family. Are we doing more damage to her with this farce?

Sam sat in one of the recliners so Piper could crawl onto his lap, and Norah started *The Polar Express*. Piper was nearly asleep before the movie finished, and Sam carried her to her room, with Norah coming to tuck her in.

"Don't stay up too late, Mommy and D-Daddy," Piper said sleepily. "S-Santa won't come while you're awake."

Sam went to his car to get the presents. When he returned, Norah was placing hers under the tree. All the lights were off except for the glowing tree, and there was a glass of wine and a beer on the coffee table.

"Norah," Sam began, "where am I sleeping?"

She stopped arranging the presents, turning to face him. "With me. I mean, I think it's what Piper will expect. And..." She paused. "I don't have anywhere else. You wouldn't be comfortable on the love seat."

His thoughts spiraled. *Shit, the last thing I want to do is share a bed with her. Is she going to expect us to make love? Because I may be less angry, but I'm not feeling any love.*

He didn't know what to say other than "Okay." There didn't seem to be any other alternative.

After the presents were all under the tree, Norah picked up the glass of wine before sitting on the love seat.

Sam sat on the recliner, sipping the beer. "I love her excitement. Can't wait to see her in the morning. Thank you for inviting me to stay."

"She needs us both," Norah said. Once they finished their drinks, she stood. "We should go to bed. She'll be awake at the crack of dawn."

Sam reluctantly climbed into bed, taking the side he'd slept on when they were together, but rolled onto his side away from her. *Damn, this is awkward, but I don't want to do anything. I don't even think I can do anything.*

Norah climbed under the covers, briefly spooning up against him from behind. When Sam didn't turn toward her, she retreated, and they fell asleep on opposite sides of the bed until early morning, when Piper came roaring into the room.

"He c-came! He c-came! There are presents under the t-tree!"

Sam opened his eyes as Norah sank deeper under the covers—she wasn't ready to get up. He climbed out of bed, reaching down to swoop up Piper for the walk to the kitchen, where he made two cups of coffee. He brought one back to Norah.

Piper could scarcely contain her excitement, hopping on one foot and then the other, waiting for Norah to come out of the bedroom.

When she did, Piper shouted, "Mommy, he brought me an animal hospital!"

Sam laughed. That was her biggest gift from Santa—too big to wrap. After they looked at everything in the stockings, Sam donned a Santa hat and distributed the gifts.

When Piper picked up the wrapped skis, she ripped the paper off and ran over to hug Sam before looking at Norah. "D-Daddy's going to teach me how to ski. We watched some races on TV." She opened the boots next before getting to the helmet, which had swirls of purple, and she immediately put it on. "It's my favorite color!" The rest of the packages from Sam contained a jacket, ski pants, goggles, and gloves. Everything was coordinated in shades of her beloved purple.

Norah chuckled. "She'll be the most stylish kid on the slopes."

They put together some of her new toys while they waited for Betsy to arrive.

While Piper played with the animal hospital, Norah looked at Sam and said softly, "I think my gifts are going to pale in comparison to yours."

"It's not a competition, Norah."

"I know. It's just..." Her voice trailed off.

"I have to keep reminding myself too." Sam shrugged. "She's happy—that's the important thing."

They heard Betsy drive up, and Piper ran to open the door. "Auntie Bets, Auntie Bets! I got skis for Christmas! And an animal hospital!"

"Wow, that's exciting!" Betsy said as she walked in. "Where are you going to ski?"

"Up where D-Daddy used to live. We're going up there t-tomorrow for Christmas."

After lunch, Piper begged to try out the skis, so Sam helped her get the boots on and then snapped her into the skis. She fell twice as he showed her how to move with them but then seemed steadier.

He led her to a small hill on the property and pointed her toward the bottom. The three adults ran down the hill as Piper slid down on the skis. At the bottom, they all fell and landed in a pile. Sam was afraid that Piper would be hurt or scared, but she laughed hysterically.

"Can I do that again, D-Daddy? P-Please, please!"

He showed her how to climb up the hill, and she made three more trips down. By the fourth time, she could stay upright at the bottom.

The daylight was waning as they made their way inside. Norah made them all hot chocolate, and Piper proclaimed, "This was the b-b-best Christmas ever!"

When Norah opened the door for them to leave, Piper walked out first. As Sam followed, Norah put her arm around him, pulling him close and leaning in to kiss him.

He froze. *What the fuck is she doing?*

Norah pulled back. "Thanks for today," she said, looking at him oddly. "It was nice."

Sam nodded. "Yes, it was." He gently kissed her on the cheek and went to his car. On the brief drive home with Piper, he wondered what Norah was thinking when she had hugged and tried to kiss him. He remembered her hand on his when she came for dinner. *She can't be thinking we should try again.*

While Piper was getting ready for bed, he remembered he wanted to send Quinn a text.

> *Sam: Merry Christmas! Hope you had a nice day.*

He sent the text with a picture of him and Piper in the snow.

> *Quinn: Thank you, I did. You and Piper look cute.*

It surprised him to get a response so quickly. He wanted to keep the conversation going, but she'd asked him not to push things, so he left it there.

They left at nine for the drive north with the car piled full of gifts for everyone and a couple of games and books that Piper wanted to bring. Piper would be the only small child there, and Sam prayed the day would be a success. He wanted her to establish a relationship with his family.

His mom and dad came out as soon as he and Piper were out of the car.

"Piper, you may not remember these grandparents, my mom and dad."

She was very shy, hiding behind Sam's legs and shaking her head.

He smiled gently. "It's been a long time since you've seen them. You can call them Gram and Grandpa. Then you won't get them confused with Nana and Pop." She nodded but still clung to his leg.

His dad kneeled, bringing himself eye level with Piper. "I think Santa left some candy in the kitchen. Would you come with us to find it?"

Piper looked questioningly at Sam.

Is he sober? Sam remembered how holidays were always an occasion to drink even more heavily than normal. But Trent's gait was steady, and his eyes were clear. Taking a deep breath, he nodded to let Piper know it was okay.

She slowly released Sam's leg, and Trent took her hand.

Laura's hand was over her mouth, tears in her eyes. "She's so beautiful," she told Sam. "Thank you for coming and for bringing Piper." When Sam reached out to embrace his mother, she held him close and murmured, "This is the best Christmas present you could have given us."

Laura took Piper's other hand, and as they walked toward the kitchen, Sam heard his father asking Piper what her favorite candy was then what Santa had brought the day before.

He exhaled as he took the packages out of the car. *I hope this goes well.* His heart was pounding, and he was terrified to lower his guard.

Sam put the presents he and Piper had brought under the tree and returned to the kitchen, where Piper was making a selection from the candy dish. "Everything smells good, Mom." He lifted the lids of the pots on the stove and peeked into the oven, where a turkey was roasting. "All my favorites from when I was a kid."

"I've stayed with almost the same menu. There might be a couple of surprises for you." She smiled.

"Did you know I do all the cooking at home?" Sam paused awkwardly. "Well, I mean, of course I do now, since there's no one else around. But even when Norah was living with me, I did all the cooking. She did the housekeeping."

His mother chuckled. "You were always much better suited to cooking than taking care of your clothes."

Joe arrived, carrying Christmas flowers for his mother. "Where are the other ladies of the family? I brought flowers for them too."

His mother had shooed Trent and Piper out of the kitchen, so Joe and Sam found them in the great room, talking about the presents under the tree with Matt and Jilly, who'd just arrived.

As Joe handed Piper a bouquet of brightly colored flowers, Sam introduced him. "Piper, this is your uncle Joe. He's my brother."

"Hi," she whispered, looking in awe at the flowers.

Joe winked at her as he extended his hand. "I'm pleased to meet you," he said with a big smile.

Piper smiled back as she shook his hand. Sam introduced Matt and Jilly to Piper, and Joe handed Jilly the last bouquet.

Sam frowned. "How did you get so charming?"

Matt nodded in agreement. "You're making the rest of us look bad."

"I know what the ladies like," Joe said. "Look at all those presents under the tree. I don't know about the rest of you, but Piper and I are ready to open them. Right, Piper?"

A shy smile wreathed her face, and she nodded.

Laura came in from the kitchen, and Sam watched as she smiled at Trent and Piper.

"Piper, let's have you sit on the couch between your grandmother and me," Trent said.

Laura sat down beside Piper then leaned over to whisper in her ear. Piper's face exploded into a grin, and she leaned against Laura.

Hmm. What did Mom say to her?

Matt handed out the presents. Through conversations he'd had with Joe and the time spent with all of them at Thanksgiving, Sam felt confident his family would appreciate what he'd gotten them.

When Trent picked one up, Piper said, "That's from us! D-d-do you need help to open it?"

"Yes, I do. Help me get this ribbon off." Once they had the paper off, he held up the book entitled *How To Be a Super Host: A Definitive Guide to Vacation Rentals.* "This is perfect! Exactly what we need."

"Mom, can you open yours from Piper and me next, please?"

She tore the paper off and found a guest book to leave at the cabin, plus a picture of him and Piper.

Piper grinned. "That's D-Daddy and me!"

"Yes—I love it! And I love the guest book. I wouldn't have thought of something like that."

Matt urged Sam to open their gift, which was a hand-carved sign that said Carpenter Brothers Carpentry. "I like Joe's idea, and I thought maybe this would make you consider it."

Sam laughed. "It's great! I love it, and I have a great spot for it. But changing careers is going to take lots of thought." He gestured at Matt. "Open our gift." Since Matt had mentioned that he had gotten into woodworking and was going to make a cradle for the baby, Sam bought him some high-quality hand tools. He'd searched for less-typical ones, and mentally he crossed his fingers, hoping Matt didn't have the ones he'd selected.

"Oh wow, these are great. I don't have any of them." Matt inspected each one. "These are outstanding—thank you so much."

Piper jumped off the couch and ran over to Jilly then grabbed one of the boxes beside her. "This is from us. C-can I help you open it?"

Jilly nodded, and they eagerly tore off the paper together. Jilly lifted out a onesie that said *The Carpenter Boys, Next Generation.*

"It's for your baby!" Piper announced. "D-Daddy had it made." Sam also gave his sister-in-law a lotion suggested by one of his female coworkers.

Jilly displayed the onesie for all of them to see and thanked him with tears in her eyes. Matt's eyes were bright as well as he nodded at Sam.

Sam reached his arms out to Piper, and she crawled into his lap. He was glad Joe had let him know the baby was a boy and that he'd stirred emotion in Matt and his wife. "Which one should we open, Pip?"

She handed him a box from his parents and watched as he opened it.

"Yes!" Sam exclaimed, holding up ski passes for Piper and himself and a gift certificate for ski lessons for Piper.

They gave Matt ski passes as well, and he smirked at Sam. "I'm going to be racing you down that mountain!"

Sam cackled. "I can't wait to beat your butt like I did in high school. We'll be back for skiing in two weeks, so get ready."

After dinner, they played Candy Land with Piper and watched a Christmas movie. Later, Matt and Jilly left to visit her parents, and after Piper fell asleep, Sam and Joe stayed up late playing gin rummy with Trent and Laura.

On their way home the next day, Piper said, "I had fun, D-D-Daddy. C-can we come up here again?"

"Yes, we can. We'll stay with my parents when we go skiing."

"Uncle Matt is funny. D-do you think he'll b-beat you racing d-down the mountain?"

"Not a chance!"

Sam couldn't stop smiling the rest of the way home.

Chapter Sixteen

An Unexpected Encounter

DURING THE FIRST WEEKEND in January, Piper woke early at his parents' house and snuck into Sam's room. "D-Daddy, is it time to get up?" she whispered in his ear.

He rubbed his eyes and reached for his phone to check the time. Her excitement was infectious, but he wanted a couple more hours of rest. "It's five thirty. We can sleep a little more. Crawl in here with me."

She squirmed for several minutes but finally fell back to sleep. They woke up again at seven thirty and dressed for skiing before going out to the kitchen, where Laura had pancakes and bacon waiting for them.

"Wow, Mom, this is nice. It's not often I have breakfast cooked for me." Sam made himself a cup of coffee and joined Piper and his father at the table.

When Piper finished eating, she climbed into her grandfather's lap and sat with him while he finished his coffee.

They arrived at the mountain at nine for her lesson, which lasted for two hours. Her group had ten kids, and Sam thought Piper did the best of all of them—though he knew he might be biased.

However, the instructor confirmed his assessment when the lesson ended. "She did well. We'll move her to intermediate for the next lesson. Are you going to ski tomorrow?"

"Yeah."

"Take her on the J-Bar. She should do okay."

Afterward, Piper and Sam did several runs down the bunny slope, and she only fell twice. Sam expected tears, but she laughed enthusiastically and bounced right back up both times. At noon, he led her to the lodge for lunch.

"Daddy, this was the b-best," she proclaimed. "I love skiing! Thank you for bringing me."

"I'm so glad you like it. We'll have some lunch, then Aunt Jilly is going to come get you so I can ski with Uncle Matt."

"Are you going to race? Will you b-beat him?"

"I hope so!" They stood in line to get food. "What was your favorite part?"

"I liked the magic carpet that t-took us up the hill. But I enjoyed skiing d-down too. I liked it all!"

Sam ruffled her hair and gave her a quick hug. "It's a lot of fun. You did a great job."

When they had their food, he led her to the dining room, which had a wall of windows looking out on the ski slopes. Round tables with seating for eight filled the space, and Sam searched for an open place to sit. Not seeing any, he was trying to think of an alternative when someone called his name.

"Sam. Hey, Sam."

Sam looked around and saw a familiar-looking man sitting at a table by himself, waving at him.

"Caden Brady," the man said. "We met in Boston. You're welcome to sit here."

Sam's mind twisted as he realized it was the doctor from Boston. *He must be here with Quinn.*

Sam led Piper to the table. "I was not expecting to run into you here."

"Quinn and I are here visiting her parents. She and her dad are on the slopes. They should come in for lunch soon."

"This is my daughter, Piper," Sam said. "She had her first lesson this morning." He turned to his daughter. "Piper, this is Dr. Brady."

Caden shook Piper's hand. "I'm pleased to meet you, Piper. Did your lesson go well?"

"Yes, I only fell twice. D-Daddy said that was great for my first t-time. After lunch, we're going to ski t-together. Do you ski?"

"I'm a beginner, just like you. I didn't take a lesson, though, because my girlfriend thought she could teach me."

Sam's mind spun. *He's enjoying referring to Quinn as his girlfriend. He for sure knows we slept together in Boston and probably knows what an ass I was when I stayed in her guest room before Christmas. I don't know if I would be this generous if the situation were reversed.*

Caden raised his hand then, and Sam saw Quinn and her father approaching the table.

Quinn's eyes opened wide. "Sam? This is a surprise."

"Sam Carpenter," her father said. "It's been a long time."

Sam stood to shake Mr. Michaels's hand, explaining that Caden had invited them to share the table. "This is my daughter, Piper. Piper, this is Quinn Michaels and her dad, Mr. Michaels. They are old friends of mine."

Piper stood and shook their hands, and they smiled and greeted her.

As Caden and Quinn went to get food, he heard her say something to Caden that ended with "How did Sam and his daughter end up sitting with you?"

Sam chuckled to himself. *I'm wondering the same thing, Quinn, exactly the same thing.* He turned to her father and told him about how he had run into Quinn in Boston.

Quinn's father looked pointedly at Sam. "Since when am I *Mr. Michaels?* The last time I saw you, I was *Hank.*"

I didn't just leave Quinn ten years ago—I left her mom and dad too. They took me in, treated me like a son, and I disappeared without a word.

Sam took a deep breath. He handed Piper his phone. "Why don't you play Emoji Blitz for a few minutes?" When she eagerly started playing, giving the phone all of her attention, he turned back to Quinn's father.

"I owe you and Mel an apology." Sam rubbed his jaw. "I made some big mistakes when Quinn and I broke up. Walking away from you with no explanation, after all you had done for me, was one of them. Quinn and I cleared the air while we were in Boston, and I hope that you and Mel can forgive me."

Mr. Michaels nodded. "I guess if Quinn can forgive you, we can as well. But I hope you know how much we missed you and how hurt we were."

His heart broke a little. "I do, and I'm sorry."

Quinn and Caden came back with their food at that moment. As they all ate and chatted, Sam watched Caden, certain the other man's hand was on Quinn's leg the entire time.

When they finished eating, Piper began bouncing in her seat. "D-do you want to see me ski?" she asked the Michaelses and Caden.

Quinn looked at Caden with a question in her eyes.

Caden nodded. "We'd love to watch you ski."

"Hank?" Sam was happy to use the older man's name. "Would you mind taking a video of Pip and me?"

Sam and Piper did a couple of runs down the bunny slope then skied back to Quinn's father to retrieve Sam's phone. Caden kept his arm around Quinn, and she leaned in close to him. Sam couldn't mistake the look of contentment on her face.

As they said goodbyes, Quinn looked at Piper and said, "I see you becoming a great racer, sweetie."

The smile that exploded over Piper's face warmed Sam's heart.

Matt and Jilly were heading toward him and Piper, but they crossed paths with Quinn, Caden, and Hank first. Sam watched as Matt gave Quinn a quick hug and introduced Jilly.

When they reached Sam, Matt said, "Hey, we ran into Quinn. Did you see her?"

"Oh yeah, we saw her."

"We ate lunch with them!" Piper said. "They're old friends of D-Daddy."

Matt burst out laughing. "Yes, they are. We want to see you ski. Will you show us before you go home with Aunt Jilly?"

Piper and Sam went to the top of the gentle slope and skied down.

"That was great, princess." Matt gave her a hug. "You'll be beating your dad and me down the slopes in no time."

Matt and Sam skied over to the chairlift, and as they rode to the top of the mountain, Matt couldn't seem to resist jabbing at

Sam. "God, Quinn looks great, even better than in high school. And a doctor for a boyfriend. She's moving up in the world."

Sam stared stoically ahead, not responding.

Matt nodded sagely. "You're still hot for her, aren't you?"

Sam continued to look at the top of the mountain. "Just shut up, Matt." Sam exited the lift and shoved off, not waiting for his brother. He was at the peak for the first time since high school, but despite being tentative to start, he quickly felt comfortable and sped down the mountain.

At the bottom, Matt skied over to him. "I'm sorry. I didn't realize Quinn was a sensitive topic."

"It's okay. We screwed up years ago, and we're different people now. I'm glad to see her happy." As he said the words, he recognized they were beginning to be true.

The brothers did several more runs, staying until the lift shut down. Before driving away from the mountain, he sent Quinn a text.

> *Sam: Please thank Caden for inviting us to sit with him. Piper enjoyed meeting all of you, and I think it made her first skiing experience even better. It's nice seeing you happy.*

Sam was setting the table for dinner when Norah arrived on Sunday. He and Piper skied all day and had been home for half an hour. The house was a mess, which would probably push Norah's buttons, but he didn't care. The weekend had been a refreshing change of pace, and Sam was thrilled by how quickly Piper took to the slopes.

He greeted her at the door. "We haven't been home long. Would you mind helping Piper with her bath? I know she's going to fall asleep soon after dinner. We were outside most of the weekend." As Norah followed Piper to the bathroom, Sam thought about how they had run into Quinn. *I have to tell Norah. And about how I saw Quinn in Boston. Not everything about Boston—God no—but at least that I ran into her.*

After a few minutes, Piper came back into the kitchen with wet hair and dressed in warm pajamas. "Can I watch t-television until dinner?"

"Yes." Sam looked around. "Where's your mom?"

"She stopped in the study."

"Oh." The study had been one of the first rooms Sam remodeled to give Norah a refuge during the renovations. It had been her favorite space in the house.

When Norah walked back into the kitchen, she wore a puzzled expression. "You put a bed in the study? Why?"

"I'm going to look for someone to rent it," Sam said. "This is a big house for just Pip and me or me alone when she's with you."

"Are you sure that's wise? What if you rent to some whack job? I don't like the idea of Piper being around someone I don't know well."

Sam closed the oven door and turned to face Norah. He took a deep breath. "Again, you need to give me some credit. I'm going to vet anyone I rent to. There's a housing need for professionals like traveling nurses." He rubbed his jaw, hoping his tone didn't reflect his aggravation at Norah for questioning his parenting decisions. Again. "That's the direction I'll be looking."

She looked thoughtful. "What if..."

Frowning, Sam met her gaze, waiting for her to finish the thought.

"What if we work things out and I move back in?"

Sam's heart twisted with an emotion he couldn't identify at the thought of her coming back. *Happiness? Anguish? Definitely not happiness. She can't really be considering it.* "We can deal with that if it happens." He took another deep breath and blew it out. "I need to tell you something..."

Just as he started to speak, Piper bounded into the kitchen. "Is d-d-dinner ready? I'm starving!"

"Yes, let's eat." Norah pulled out a chair. "I'm not surprised you're hungry after being outside all weekend."

As soon as they sat down, Piper started jabbering to her mother about the weekend. She described the breakfast Laura had made for them, her lesson, the magic carpet, baking cookies with Jilly. Then she said, "And we ate lunch in the lodge with friends of D-Daddy. Dr. Brady saw us looking for a table, and he invited us to sit with him. He was there with his girlfriend, Quinn, and her father. D-Daddy knew her in high school."

Sam's heart sank. *This is not going to go well.*

Norah looked at Sam, eyebrows raised. "You ran into Quinn? Were you going to tell me?"

He tried to smile. "I knew the town crier would do it."

"Dr. Brady recognized D-Daddy from B-Boston," Piper continued. "We wouldn't have had anywhere to sit if he hadn't seen us. They were nice. Mr. Michaels took a video of us skiing. Show her the video, D-Daddy."

As Sam was finding the video, Norah said, in an odd voice, "You saw her in Boston?"

While Norah was pretending to watch the video, Sam murmured, "We'll talk about it later."

"D-did I s-say s-something wrong?" Piper asked, looking at her mother with concern.

Sam shook his head. "Not at all. Mom is just surprised we saw someone I know." The atmosphere at the table remained strained for the rest of the meal, and when they finished, he said, "Piper, you and Mommy go into the living room to read. I'll be in when I'm done in the kitchen."

After a few minutes, Norah called out, "You were right about her being tired. I'm going to take her to bed."

After tucking Piper in, Norah returned to the kitchen and poured herself a glass of wine. She stood at the counter sipping it, watching while he finished cleaning up. She didn't say a word, but Sam could sense her displeasure. He went to Piper's room to kiss her goodnight, returned to the kitchen for a beer, then followed Norah to the living room.

"You spent time with Quinn in Boston?" she asked. "You didn't tell me anything about that."

"I didn't tell you anything about Boston. You had moved out."

"Mmm. And you weren't talking to me. What was it like seeing her?"

"Awkward at first." Sam sighed and relayed the story about getting to the conference late and sitting next to Quinn. "We had dinner. We caught up."

"You only saw her that one time?"

Sam looked away. "No, I saw her every day I was there. I was a wreck, Norah—I needed someone to talk to. You always told me I had unfinished business with her. Well, we talked about the end of our relationship, and we cleared up a lot of questions. So, you should be happy. I have nothing unfinished now."

She snorted. "Not sure 'happy' is the word I'd use."

They sat in strained silence for a few minutes.

Sam tried again. "Did you hear the part where Piper said her boyfriend was with her? All there is between Quinn and me is friendship."

"I have to wonder. Is this why you wanted nothing to do with me on Christmas Eve? Why you wouldn't even kiss me?"

He met her gaze. "Sex will not fix what's wrong between us. Last summer proved that."

"You were plenty hot for me then, before you spent a week with Quinn." Norah finished her wine, and Sam saw her hands were shaking.

He shook his head. "Norah, we talked. She listened to me lament about you leaving, and we worked through old hurts. I didn't *spend* a week with her." At least all of this was true, even if it wasn't the whole truth. Sam couldn't—wouldn't—admit to Norah that he had slept with Quinn in Boston and in this house. Not right now. *Maybe when things calm down, maybe in the future, but I can't throw it at her now when she just needs to come to terms with me not wanting to get back together.* "I just... are you really thinking you and I are going to be able to work things out?"

"My lease is only six months." She shrugged. "I thought maybe the longer time apart would fix things. But now I don't know."

"We can't keep doing this on-and-off dance. We have to get it right, whether that means we are together or apart. But I don't see us being together anymore like we were." He paused. "I'm going to start seeing a therapist. As a matter of fact, my first appointment is tomorrow."

She blinked back tears. "So you would never consider getting back together? And you're keeping things from me, like seeing Quinn?"

Dammit, Norah never cries. This is a mess. "I probably should have told you about running into Quinn, but there really hadn't been a good time to drop that on you. But now... I think you should leave. We've said all we need to."

She stumbled toward the door and turned to look at him. "I can't believe this." She left without another word.

Sam went to the kitchen for another beer. He'd known from the minute he introduced Piper to Quinn and her dad that she would tell Norah about it. He hadn't asked Pip to keep it quiet because he didn't want her to feel like she needed to hide things from either him or Norah.

His stomach roiled. There was an element of untruth in what he told Norah, but he hadn't spent the entire week sleeping with Quinn. Admitting what had happened between them would have made everything...

"D-Daddy?" He turned to see Piper standing at the end of the hall.

"Pip, what are you doing up?"

"I heard you and M-Mommy t-talking." A tear rolled down her cheek.

He opened his arms, and she ran into them.

"D-does M-mommy n-not like Q-Quinn?" Piper asked, sniffling. "I thought she was n-nice."

This was the worst her stutter had been in months, and it broke his heart. "Mommy doesn't really know Quinn."

Sam held Piper, trying to figure out how to explain Norah's behavior. "Do you know what jealousy is?"

Pip shook her head.

"It's kind of like this. If you had a pony, you'd love it and be thrilled with it. But if you found out your best friend had two ponies, that might make you sad and angry. You would wonder why you can't have two ponies." He paused and looked down at her. "That's what jealousy is. It's that feeling of wanting what someone else has. Do you understand?"

"I th-think so."

"So, Mommy is a little jealous of Quinn because I knew her a long time ago, when I was in high school and college. Mommy wishes she had known me back then."

Piper nodded. "Was Quinn your girlfriend?"

"Yes, and I think Mommy wishes she was the only girlfriend I'd ever had. It surprised her tonight to learn that we saw Quinn this weekend, and that I had seen her when I was in Boston. You know how sometimes a surprise makes you cry or makes you angry?" When she nodded, Sam sighed. "That's what happened tonight. Once Mommy thinks about it for a bit, she won't be angry anymore."

"I shouldn't have t-told her that we had l-lunch with th-them."

"No, Pip. You were telling her about the weekend, and lunch was part of it. Never think you must hide something just so Mommy or I don't get upset." He hugged her and picked her up. "Let's get you back into bed. You have school tomorrow, and you can tell all your friends about how you went skiing."

After putting her back to bed, Sam sat on the couch to finish his beer, his stomach still in knots. *I really fucked this up. But when was I going to tell Norah about seeing Quinn? We were hardly talking until a couple of weeks ago.*

He took a gulp of beer. *I hate she was blindsided, but my bigger concern is Piper. We had such a great weekend. I don't want that to be tainted by a past that has no bearing on my future.*

Chapter Seventeen

It's Not Your Fault

AS HE APPROACHED THE purple door at the cream-colored Victorian house, Sam muttered to himself, "Jesus, I'm late. I should have gotten gas last night."

He'd done enough counseling with Norah to know that therapists kept to a tight schedule, and he'd just wasted part of his hour. The directory posted in the entrance directed him to the second floor for the office of Archibald Ovitt, Psy.D.—Jesse told Sam they'd been in the same doctoral program and thought Dr. Ovitt would be a good fit, but the reassurance did nothing to calm Sam's heart. It pounded from the stress of being late and the idea of laying himself bare.

He'd barely sat down in the waiting room when the office door opened.

"Sam?" A man dressed casually in a black Henley and khakis extended his hand. "Archie Ovitt. Come on in."

The office looked like the ones Sam had gone to for couples' counseling and for family counseling: a couch, an overstuffed chair, a desk, and another door on the opposite wall.

Sam took a deep breath. "Where should I sit?"

"Wherever you'll feel comfortable."

Sam hesitated then walked to the couch, sat down, and brought his left foot to his right knee. "Should I call you Dr. Ovitt?"

"Archie is fine." He pulled the office chair away from the desk and sank into it. "What brings you in, Sam?"

"Did Jesse tell you about my situation?"

"Nope, just said he had a friend looking for a therapist," Archie said easily. "And I wouldn't have listened anyway. I want to hear it from you."

Sam's left leg shook even with his foot firmly anchored to his knee. "My partner moved out of our house in November, and I'm not dealing with it very well."

"The separation wasn't something you wanted?"

"It was something that needed to happen, but the timing surprised me. I had work obligations in Boston for a week, and she left while I was gone." Sam moved his foot to the floor and rested his hands on his thighs, hoping to quell the trembling. "Norah took everything she'd brought into the house. Which left me with a couch, a recliner, and the television. Not much to show for thirty-one years of living."

Archie nodded. "Why do you say it needed to happen?"

"Our six-year-old daughter started stuttering over a year ago. The family therapist we were seeing thinks it's a reaction to the tension between us."

"Do you know what causes that tension?"

Sam shrugged. "I'm messy, and Norah's a neat freak." He chuckled ruefully, adding, "Obviously, there's more to it than that."

"Can you elaborate?"

Sam thought about it. "Are you married? Or in a long-term relationship?"

Archie cocked his head. "I am."

"Have you ever gone through a phase where just the sound of your partner breathing makes you want to run out the door screaming?"

"We're supposed to be talking about your relationship, not mine." Archie's eyes narrowed a little.

Sam shrugged. "I just want to know that you'll understand what I'm saying."

"Pretty sure I'll understand."

"Okay. We've gone through periods like that, where every-thing the other one does is irritating to the nth degree. Then it would pass, and we'd go through periods where just watching Norah put her socks on would fill me with joy. You know what I mean?" Sam looked at Archie, who nodded. "I can't remember the last time there was a sock moment. But I can recall plenty of run-out-the-door ones."

"You say you can't remember any good moments," Archie said. "How far back are we talking?"

Sam brought his foot back to his knee and drummed his fingers on it. "Piper started stuttering not this past summer but the one before... so what's that, a year and a half? Norah and I had been going to couples' counseling for a year before that. We switched to family counseling after the stutter started." His stomach was tied in knots.

"So you've been having problems for about two and a half years?"

"Longer than that. It wasn't like we recognized right away that we weren't getting along. It dragged on for months before we realized we needed help."

"And in all that time, have you identified any specific issues?"

Sam scoffed. "Yeah. I'm messy, and she's a neat freak." He shook his head. "We just drive each other crazy." He bowed his head and massaged his forehead. The months that he spent at his friend's cabin during the summer came to mind. "I may have misspoken."

He told Archie about the summer and how he and Norah had gotten along better when he was living there. "If we're not living together, things are fine. We've discussed living apart but still being committed to each other, if that makes sense."

"It does. Some couples find an alternative living arrangement like that can work."

Sam looked up and shook his head. "I don't want to live that way. And she's been gone for two months, but the good moments haven't returned, so I don't think that's a solution."

"Do you see your daughter?"

"Of course. She's with me half the time."

"Has the separation helped her?"

Sam knew Archie was asking about the stutter. "Not yet."

"Often when there's tension between partners, if they separate they feel better, not being under that constant stress. That's not true for you?"

"I've never lived alone. I'm... having a hard time when Piper isn't with me."

"How long were you and Norah together?"

"Eight years."

"Married?"

"No."

"Let's put a pin in that to come back to. So, you got together when you were twenty-three. What were your living situations before then? Did you live with your parents?"

"God no." Sam recoiled. "Except for a brief period when I was twenty-one, I haven't lived full-time with my parents since high school."

"Roommates?"

"Not exactly. For a couple of years during college, I spent most of my time at my girlfriend's parents' house. When we split, I moved in with a woman I'd become friends with, and when that ended, Norah and I moved in together." Sam hated having to admit that he'd moved from one woman to another with no break between, but it was the truth. "I've never *not* been in a relationship. And I know how that sounds."

"How do you think it sounds?"

Sam shrugged. "Like I don't know how to be alone."

"Which you admitted you're having a hard time with. Have you developed any coping mechanisms?"

"Yeah." He snorted. "Beer."

"To excess?"

"Sometimes. But not when Piper is with me."

"Where do you drink? You're not driving drunk, are you?"

"Mostly at home." Sam's leg started jiggling again. "A few weeks ago, Norah and I went to mediation, and I went to a bar to decompress afterward. I ended up calling a former girlfriend, and she let me sleep in her guest room."

"That was generous."

"Yeah." Silence dragged out between them, and Sam wished Archie would say something. "The girl? The one whose parents I stayed with? I ran into her at that work thing in Boston. We hadn't seen each other in ten years, and we spent time together. I was shitty to her when we broke up, and I needed to make that right."

"Shitty because you'd started dating someone else?"

"Partly. She was away at college. We took a break, and I got caught up with a woman I met. We didn't have sex, but we might as well have. Quinn wanted to end the break and told me she hadn't been with anyone. I found out she'd lied about that, and I ended our relationship. But I put the blame all on her. I didn't admit what I'd done." He sighed. "We ironed all that out in Boston. That's who I called."

"Just friends?"

Sam's face reddened. "We, uh, we tried for more, but she thinks I'm not over Norah. And she's involved with someone else now. Truthfully, I made a pass at her when she took me home. It wasn't my finest hour. That's when I asked Jesse to help me find someone."

"You recognized the inappropriate behavior and want to change. That's all positive. Have you made amends with her?"

"More or less." Sam answered with a shrug.

Archie nodded. "Tell me about Norah."

"She has an advanced degree in environmental science and heads a new agency tasked with ensuring compliance with state climate initiatives. She's beautiful, loves our daughter, and wants to save the planet."

"Sounds like an accomplished individual. How would she describe you if she were here?"

Sam scratched his head. "She'd say I'm scattered, bouncing from one project to another, always late, and won't clean up after myself."

"Everything you said about her was positive," Archie said. "Surely, she'd have some positives about you."

"I'm an excellent cook and a fully involved dad. Although she has a hard time giving me credit for that one." When Archie cocked his head, Sam shrugged. "Norah goes to work early and comes home late, so before she left, I was totally in charge of Piper before school and at the end of the workday. And I did a good job, but I don't feel like that was recognized."

He paused. "I have no idea how she's handling mornings on the days she has Pip. That's bugged me since she left. She was obsessed with arriving at work early when we were together."

"You only have one child?"

Sam nodded. "Norah believes overpopulation is a problem, so…"

"Do you believe that?"

Sam gazed out the window, trying to craft an answer. "I…" He grimaced. "I rarely get asked what I believe. I have two brothers, and I enjoyed growing up with siblings. I'm sad that Pip is missing out on that."

Archie nodded. "Have you deferred to Norah in other areas?"

Sam pondered the question for a moment. "Nothing comes to mind, but probably. She's super intelligent. Why wouldn't I?"

Archie leaned back a little in his chair. "How did you get together?"

"I'm a project manager for an economic-development firm, and she consulted on one of my jobs."

"Do you have a degree?"

"Yeah, a BS in architecture. I'm working on a master's in project management."

"So, you're educated, yet you seem to consider yourself lesser compared to her."

He scoffed. "Norah grew up in an affluent family in New York City, then she went to a swanky college. Now she heads a department for the state. I grew up in a small town in the Northeast Kingdom. My relatives work in factories and other blue-collar jobs. I barely made it through high school and went to a small college in Maine. There's really no comparison between us."

"What attracted her to you?"

Sam chuckled. "I'm good in bed."

Archie smiled. "That's an important component in relationships. Did it suffer as tension grew between you?"

"Not really. Honestly, sex was our go-to way to settle any disagreements, which of course really settled nothing. I get that. But when Norah moved out, my desire for her evaporated."

"That's understandable. Let's go back to the drinking. Was that an issue when you were together?"

He shook his head. "We enjoyed a drink at the end of the day or in social settings, but I wasn't prone to getting drunk."

"And you are now?"

Sam nodded.

"Did that start when you returned to the empty house?"

"Kinda." Sam rubbed his jaw. "I got drunk in Boston the night I told Quinn the truth about our breakup."

"You've mentioned Quinn a couple of times. She's important to you?"

"I met her when I was a senior in high school and she was a sophomore. We started dating just before I left for college. She's the first woman I loved." Sam paused. "She's an issue between Norah and me. Norah felt I had unfinished business with her." He told Archie what had happened the night before.

"Does Norah have issues with other women you've dated?"

"Not at all. We've even joked about different women being interested in me or men being interested in her. But about Quinn? Radioactive."

"Our hour is almost over. Do you want to meet again?"

Sam thought for a minute. "Yeah. One more thing. Back in Boston, Quinn mentioned ADHD as a reason for my scattered behavior, and Jesse told me to mention it to you."

Archie thought for a minute. "I'm going to email you a questionnaire. It's lengthy, so tackle it when you've got a chunk of time, then send it back to me. I can prescribe meds based on what I see from your answers." He gave Sam a smile. "I'll see you in a couple of weeks."

Two weeks later, Sam stood in front of the purple door, smiling as he looked at his watch. Five minutes early. He sat in the waiting room, collecting his thoughts, until Archie opened the door to his office.

"Greetings." Archie waited for Sam to enter and sit on the couch before taking his place on the rolling office chair. "How are you doing?"

"I was early today. That's an unusual occurrence for me."

Archie tilted his head, clearly inviting Sam to say more.

"My focus began to improve as soon as I took one pill from the prescription you gave me," Sam said. "That was surprising. I expected it to take several weeks."

"I'm glad to hear that. We can tinker with the dosage and should get your primary doctor involved, for at least a physical. I know some behavioral strategies we can talk about too." He paused. "I wanted to get you started on something to see if it made a difference, but meds will now be an ongoing part of our discussion going forward. Do you exercise?"

"Yeah, I run, although that's challenging this time of year. I'm getting back into skiing."

"Any issues with finding excuses not to pursue those things?"

Sam let out a self-deprecating breath. "I can be the king of excuses."

"The meds should help with that, and regular exercise can have a powerful effect on your mental state, so I'd encourage you to fit that into your schedule." Archie studied the pad of paper on his lap. "You had a strong reaction when I asked you about living with your parents. I'd like to hear more about that."

"My dad sank heavily into alcohol when I was in high school." Sam shook his head at the memories. "He was a mean drunk—not physically but a lot of verbal abuse. When I started dating Quinn, which he saw as an act of defiance, I more or less moved into her house. Her parents gave me a safe haven. I went back to my parents' house after she left for college because I was doing an internship locally and it felt weird to be at her house when she was gone. I lasted three months and haven't lived with them since."

A bottle of water sat on the table next to the couch. Sam unscrewed the top and took a long swallow. "I've been estranged from my whole family until just a couple of months ago."

"Even your brothers? You said you were happy to have grown up with them."

Sam nodded.

"Did you reconcile around the same time that Norah moved out?"

Sam thought about it and shrugged. "A few weeks after."

"Did she play a part in the estrangement?"

"Not really. I was already distancing myself from them when we moved in together. I described the dark moods and the alcoholism, and she supported my decision to stay away from family gatherings."

"How did the reconciliation come about?"

Sam described Thanksgiving and the furniture then relayed the story Joe told him about Trent getting sober before relating Trent's visit. "Piper and I stayed overnight at Christmas then again when we went skiing. I never would have done that before." He sighed. "Piper didn't even know them."

"How do you feel about that?"

"I'm appalled that my daughter was six years old before she knew my family."

"Sometimes we need to remove ourselves from toxic situations to protect our well-being. It sounds like that's what you did." Archie paused. "Did your brothers do the same?"

"Not as completely as I did, but yes, to some degree, they stopped having contact with our father."

"Your mom and your brothers were residual damage. That isn't your fault."

Sam took another swallow of water. This was the first time anyone had absolved him from his behavior toward his family. His eyes filled, and he wiped his hand across his face.

Archie rolled his chair to the desk, picked up a box of tissues, and handed them to Sam. He gave Sam a few minutes to pull himself together before asking another question. "Are you happy to have them in your life again?"

"Oh yeah. Especially Joe." Sam blew his nose. "We're a year apart and we were close growing up. It's good to see his texts or get a call from him out of the blue. Matt—he's the youngest—is the same pain in the ass that he was when we were growing up." He laughed. "My mother never gave up on me. It's good to know I'm not hurting her anymore. And Piper loves all of them. I..." Sam stopped.

When Sam didn't continue, Archie asked, "What's bothering you?"

"I'm afraid it's not going to last. Every time I visit, I expect my father to be drunk. I'm a ball of anxiety until I see that he's sober."

"You went through significant trauma. That will not disappear overnight."

Sam's eyes went wide. "I hope to God it does at some point!"

"It may or may not," Archie said. "The anxiety will probably decrease each time that you have a positive interaction with him, however."

"Can I get up?"

Archie grinned. "Of course. You can do whatever makes you comfortable in this space."

Sam walked over to the window and took several deep breaths. He turned to Archie. "I didn't know this would be so hard to talk about." He walked back to the couch and finished the bottle of water.

"We have about fifteen minutes left. There's one more thing I'd like to talk about before you leave. You said Trent was a mean drunk. Are you?"

Sam took a breath. "Probably only to myself."

"How does that manifest?"

Sam rubbed his jaw. "I don't know. I never wanted to be a person who drinks like this. In my twenties, I'd go to bars and make one or two beers last the whole night. I don't want to be this person."

"You used the word 'alcoholic' to describe your father. Does that term fit you?"

"No. I don't drink at all when I have Piper." He replayed the time since Norah left, remembering the first night she came to dinner and how happy he'd been to have only had one beer after she left. Shaking his head, he corrected himself. "I don't drink to excess when Piper is with me. There's a difference between social drinking and problem drinking, isn't there?"

"Do you think so?"

Sam's foot started to jiggle as it had during his first visit. "You can be very frustrating."

"That's why I make the big bucks." Archie gave him a kind smile. "Give it some thought, and we'll pick up here the next time."

Chapter Eighteen
A Ski Weekend

SAM WAITED IN THE drive at the cabin and smiled as he watched Jesse's Suburban come to a stop beside him. The doors opened, and children poured out. Piper had begged to ride with Janey, so Sam carried the equipment, happy to grant her wishes when he could. He called over to Jesse and Caitlin. "Do you want to see the place before we unload the cars?" When they nodded, he led them inside.

"Ooh, Sam," Caitlin exclaimed. "This *is* nice. You were holding back on us."

"You should have seen it before. The transformation is amazing, and it's not done yet." Sam led them to the bunk room. "This is where Diego, Antonia, and Janey will sleep." He started to move to the other bedroom when Janey grabbed his arm.

"Wait. Can't Piper sleep here with us?"

"I thought she'd be upstairs with me."

Both girls looked at him with puppy-dog eyes. "Pleeease," they begged, looking from one parent to another.

Toni spoke up next. "They can share the big bed. I'll sleep in the top bunk, and Diego can have the bottom."

Diego rolled his eyes. "Can I sleep on the couch out there? I don't want to share a room with those three girls. Or even just two of them."

After a quick consultation, the grown-ups agreed to the sleeping arrangement, but Caitlin had the last word. "You girls can't be up giggling all night long. And we need help to unpack the car."

With everything out of the car, they hopped back in the Suburban for the drive to Sam's parents' house. The kids jabbered in the back seat while Sam sat quietly in the front seat, only talking to give Jesse directions. His mother had invited the whole troupe for dinner as soon as Sam told her about their ski weekend. Even after the sessions with Archie, he still became anxious when he thought about spending time with his father. He had never introduced any of his friends to his parents—this was unfamiliar territory.

Laura and Trent walked out as soon as the car arrived, just as they had done at Christmas. Piper jumped out of the car first, throwing her arms around her grandparents, then pulling them over to her friends. "This is m-my grandparents." She waved her hand. "This is Janey, T-T-Toni, and D-Diego."

Sam joined them. "Mom, Dad, these are my friends Jesse and Caitlin Ortega. I guess Pip already took care of introducing the kids. Jesse, Cait, my parents, Laura and Trent."

Trent grasped Jesse's hand. "It's good to meet you."

Jesse nodded. "Thanks for inviting us. You may regret it. These cowboys can be a lot."

Laura smiled. "We raised three cowboys. I'm sure we can handle yours. Let's get inside. It's cold out here."

At dinner, the talk centered on the next day. "Have you skied before?" Laura was looking at Jesse and Caitlin.

"I grew up in Maine, and I skied at Sunday River. But it's been years."

"It'll come right back to you. It did for Sam and Matt, from what I've heard." Trent turned to Jesse. "How about you?"

Jesse shook his head. "I grew up in Florida. No snow there. And I've got a bad knee."

"He played professional baseball." Diego was proud of his dad and let everyone know about his accomplishments. "That's how his knee got torn up."

Jesse flashed a warning look at his son, but before he could say anything, Trent spoke up.

"Ortega." Trent cocked his head. "You played for Tampa Bay. I was watching that game where you were injured. That was brutal."

"Yeah."

Sam knew Jesse disliked talking about his career and its premature end. He searched for a way to change the subject, but his mother beat him to it.

"The lodge is very comfortable, with nice food options. There's nothing wrong with enjoying the day from there. It's certainly my preference today, after years of being out in the cold when the boys were growing up."

After they finished eating, Piper pulled Trent into a game of Candy Land with Janey and Toni. The game lasted until they went home, and Sam snuck glances at his father laying outstretched on the floor, reacting to the girls' glee anytime they could send him back to the beginning. *I have to go back a really long way to find a memory like that. I'm so glad Piper is seeing this version of him.*

First thing the next morning, a technician fitted Diego and Janey with skis and boots before turning to Jesse. "How tall are you?"

"I'm going to pass. I'll just spectate today." He looked toward Sam as the kids clamored for him to try it.

Sam spoke up. "Your mom and I are going to have our hands full keeping track of the four of you. We can't be digging your dad out of a snowbank."

The kids laughed, and Sam took a step closer to Jesse. "You'll come out and watch while we get them started, won't you?" He kept his voice low so only Jesse could hear. "I get it, man, but I think they'd like you to see them."

Jesse nodded. "Of course."

Sam fought with self-doubt as he worked with Diego and Janey, who had never been on skis before. *I didn't need to tell Jesse to come out here. He would have anyway.* "That's the way, Janey. Remember to keep your knees bent and relax." *I was thinking about how much I longed for my dad to come to my races.* "I think you guys are ready to ride the magic carpet." He watched as the lift attendant guided them, then as he stepped on, turned his head back to Jesse. "We'll be back down here in a flash."

Diego fell as they reached the bottom and struggled with how to position the skis so he could stand but ultimately bounced up unhurt. Sam could see how much Janey wanted to razz him, but he also saw Caitlin's face and watched Janey change course.

"That was so much fun," she exclaimed. "Are we going to go again?"

Caitlin nodded, and they made several more trips up the slope, eventually switching over to the steeper side. Jesse watched the entire time, and at lunchtime, he told his wife, "I'll take them inside if you and Sam want to go to the top."

Caitlin exchanged a glance with Sam, and he answered for both of them. "This weekend is for the kids. I don't need to go any higher."

Piper tugged on his sleeve. "What about the J-B-B-Bar?"

"You think they're ready for that?" Sam smiled at her.

Piper nodded so enthusiastically her whole body shook.

Caitlin laughed. "Let's have some lunch first."

As they ate their sandwiches, Piper told Janey how they had sat with Quinn on their first trip. "I t-t-told Mommy about it, and she was m-mad. Quinn was D-Daddy's girlfriend a long time ago, and my m-mother is jealous."

Piper may have been talking to Janey, but the entire table heard, and all eyes turned toward Sam except for Piper's and Janey's, who were enjoying their conversation. Piper continued. "I thought Quinn was nice. She t-told me I was going to be a great racer."

"Wow," Janey breathed.

Piper's eyes sparkled. "And she was pretty."

Sam could see Jesse and Caitlin holding back laughter, and as the blush on his cheeks faded, he cleared his throat. "You girls need to eat your sandwiches if you want to go back out."

"Can I bail on this afternoon?" Diego looked from one parent to the other. "There's an arcade upstairs."

Toni gave him a side glance. "Afraid to fall again? I..."

"Antonia!" Jesse's tone left no doubt. "I imagine each of you is going to fall at some point today. I'm going to watch from the windows this afternoon. And yes, you may go to the arcade, Diego."

After a quick conference, Caitlin led the three girls outside, and Sam stayed in the lodge with Jesse. "Think I need a babysitter?"

"No. Just some company." The two men found chairs in front of the large expanse of glass that looked out on the slopes. "I had no idea Cait was such a skilled skier."

Jesse guffawed. "Me either. She mentioned it a couple of times but didn't make a big deal of it. Quinn's pretty, huh?"

"I have no secrets." Sam shrugged. "It's okay. I love seeing Pip having a good time at something I loved back in the day." He pointed to the glass. "There they go." They watched until the girls and Caitlin were out of sight. "Hey, earlier—I didn't mean to imply that you wouldn't watch. You're a terrific father. I was thinking about my own and how he never came to any of my races."

"I figured that. The man we saw last night, lying on the floor and playing games with the girls, wasn't much like the man you've told me about."

"I know." Sam cocked his head. "You believe what I told you about him? Don't you?"

"Come on. Of course I do. I know firsthand how substance abuse affects personality. What a gift that he got himself together. Is it getting easier for you?"

"Slowly."

Chapter Nineteen

A Good Day

A WEEK LATER, SAM pushed back from his desk after over two hours, comparing the final punch lists for the company's latest project. He squeezed his eyes shut to rest them from the tedium of studying the two screens in front of him. *Geesh, it isn't even my project.*

Shaking his head sharply, he opened his eyes and picked up his phone. He scrolled to the ad he'd been working on to attract a tenant for his extra room. Norah's concerns when she saw the bed in the study had rattled him, and now he was questioning his decision to rent the room. The bed had come back with him and Piper after Christmas. And tonight, his parents were bringing a bureau while he was still wrestling with whether to go forward.

When Laura had called saying they wanted to give him a bureau, she had asked what color the walls were, and Sam knew she had something up her sleeve. In a rare unguarded moment, he'd invited them to come for dinner. His mother had never seen his house, and Trent had only been there that one night back in the fall. Sam was excited to show off his cooking skills, which had moved far beyond the basics that Laura had taught him and his brothers. As it had so often since Thanksgiving, apprehension about what version of Trent would show up tinged his excitement.

His mind drifted back to Archie telling him the years-long estrangement from his family wasn't his fault. Four little words that Sam had replayed over and over again since their last session. And every time he heard them, he felt pieces of the wall he'd built around himself falling away.

His office phone buzzed, and Sam absently picked it up, still thinking about Archie's words. "Carpenter."

"Hey, Sam." Larry James, the company CEO, greeted him. "I wondered if you're free for a few minutes."

"I'm just finishing up those punch lists. What do you need?" Larry had only been in his position for a couple of months, and Sam hadn't had many interactions with him.

"Could you come to my office?"

"Sure, I'll be right there." Sam hung up the phone and slowly stood. *Why do I feel like I'm being summoned to the principal's office?* He walked down the long hallway, and when he entered, Larry motioned toward the empty chairs that faced his desk.

"I don't think you've been here since I started, have you?"

"No. It's been kind of busy." Sam's feeling of being in the principal's office increased.

"It has. That's what I want to talk to you about. I appreciate the way you've stepped up since Anderson has been out."

The company had three leads that the project managers worked under, and one of them, Anderson, had called out sick after the Christmas holiday. His project was in its last stages, and Larry asked Sam to oversee its completion even though he wasn't part of Anderson's team. Other than the ski weekends, work overwhelmed Sam throughout the month as he scrambled to complete the added project while keeping up with his own. "The job was at a crucial point. We all did what was needed."

"Everyone contributed, but I know you were the one who kept it going. I haven't been here long, but I've developed a sense of what's going on. I know how many things can go wrong in the last few weeks of a project, and you shepherded it through without an incident. Thank you."

Sam squirmed in his seat, not accustomed to praise like this. "Just doing my job."

A faint smile crossed Larry's face, and then it was gone. "Anderson's not coming back."

Sam cocked his head, waiting to hear if Larry was going to elaborate. This absence wasn't Anderson's first, and there had been rumors about mental health issues. When Larry didn't immediately continue, Sam asked, "Is he okay?"

"Yes." Larry nodded. "He's found something that fits his skill set better. The board and I met this morning, and we want to offer you the lead position." The smile that had been barely there a few minutes earlier broke free.

Sam had been leaning forward in the chair, and he slumped back. "That wasn't what I was expecting when you called me in here."

"What were you expecting?"

"I don't know." Sam grinned.

"I understand if you need some time to think about it."

"No." Sam shook his head. "I want this. I've wanted it for a couple of years, but I didn't think there would be any changes for a while. You know I don't have my master's?"

"I know you're only four courses away from it."

He's looked into me. "That's right. I'm taking two now. I'll finish in the fall."

"You've demonstrated enough for us to know that you're the right person for the job." Larry shuffled some papers on his desk. "The other leads know we're offering this to you, and they're on board. I didn't want to make any changes when I first arrived, but I've been watching, and I think there are things we can do better. I want you three leads to get together and configure your teams. You all know who works well together, and I'm eager to see how you decide to set things up."

Sam sat silently, absorbing the news. *The job I want and carte blanche to set up my team. This is a good day.*

Larry slid apiece of paper toward him. "This is what we're offering for your salary. It'll go up when you finish your coursework."

Sam looked at the figure and swallowed hard. It represented a significant increase over what he was currently making. He looked up at Larry. "That works."

Larry stood and extended his hand. "Fantastic. I think the other leads are ready to meet with you and get the reorganization started."

Sam shook his hand and walked toward the door. When he entered the hallway, one of the clerical staff waved, beckoning him to the break room. He found the entire office gathered there, ready to congratulate him. The one accessory they all wore was a wide smile. There was a variety of pizzas and cupcakes from his favorite bakery on the table. The lead he'd been working under grabbed his hand. "So happy for you, Sam. You deserve it. The work you've done this month has been incredible." That scene replayed over and over again, and Sam struggled to remember a time when he'd felt so valued.

An hour later, Sam sat at his desk, stunned. *Lead. I can't wait to tell Jesse. And my parents.* He stood and shoved his chair in. The punch list was done, and everything else could wait until the next day. He would take the afternoon off so he could be ready when his parents arrived.

Sam walked out to their truck, and as he hugged his mother, she said, "Have you had a good day? Anything exciting happen?" It was the same way she had greeted him and his brothers every afternoon.

"Same old, same old." That had been his response throughout high school. "Let's get that bureau inside. I'll give you the tour, then we can eat." He was enjoying the anticipation of sharing his news with them.

The bureau coordinated with the bed, and once it was in place, his mother opened the large shopping bag she was carrying. "I brought you some things to dress the room up a little." She pulled out an autumn-colored patchwork quilt that would coordinate with the caramel walls. "Grab the other side, Trent, so we can put it on evenly." Next, she brought out coordinating pillows and then fluffy white towels. "Dad told me the bedroom you're going to rent has a bathroom. You want it to look as good as possible. You know, to sell the space."

"Thanks, Mom." Sam chuckled. "I appreciate it."

Sam showed his mother the house and shared the "before" pictures with her, just as he had with his father. She admired everything, and Sam basked in her approval. Just before they sat down to eat, he said, "I'm glad you're here tonight. I had a fantastic day, and I'm excited to tell you about it."

Chapter Twenty

Archie Earns His Money

SAM SAT IN ARCHIE'S waiting room with his leg jiggling at almost ten minutes after two, the first time that Archie had been late welcoming him in. That was doing nothing to ease his nerves. He didn't have an answer to the question Archie had posed at their last session, and he wondered where this discussion would lead.

The door opened, and Archie appeared, looking less put together than at their first two meetings. "Sorry for the delay. Come on in."

Sam took his usual place on the couch. "Problem?"

Archie waved his hand. "A client who was having a hard time. I try to stay on schedule, but I'm not going to kick someone out the door if they're in crisis." He rolled his office chair into place. "That being said, your session will have to be short today so I can get back on track. I'll adjust your bill." He grinned at Sam. "Unless, of course, you fall apart with ten minutes left." Archie took a breath and shook his head. "That was a lame attempt at a joke. We'll go wherever we need to."

Sam wondered if anything he said would cause Archie distress, the way the previous client obviously had. "I'm good with ending at our regular time."

Archie nodded. "How's your life been since I last saw you? You went on the ski weekend with your friends, didn't you? Did you see your family while you were there?"

"The trip went well. We had dinner with my parents. And before you ask, yes, I had the same anxiety I always do, but it went well. He lay on the floor playing games with my daughter and her friends. That was so cool to see." Sam took a deep breath and then smiled. "I have more news. I got a promotion at work." He described the day and what the recognition meant to him.

"It's great to see you like this. I have something I want to go back to. Do you want to make me earn my money today? Or leave you in your good mood?"

"No. Let's go."

"You and Norah aren't married. Did you discuss it?"

"Norah doesn't believe in marriage."

Archie's mouth quirked.

Sam sighed. "I know. You want to know what I believe."

Archie nodded.

"I grew up thinking I'd get married. I proposed when Norah told me she was pregnant, and she said we hadn't been together long enough." Sam looked at the other man, knowing the next question. "We'd been together eight months."

"Was the pregnancy a surprise?"

"It surprised me." Sam remembered how shocked he'd been when Norah told him they were going to have a baby. It had taken him a few days to absorb the news and become excited by it. *I need to tell him what happened after the first proposal.*

"When I proposed, Norah didn't just turn me down—she told me she was thinking about terminating the pregnancy." Sam took a deep breath, trying to calm the distress he always felt when he remembered that moment. "We argued for a week over that. Until we heard Piper's heartbeat. And then I knew I'd won." He looked down and then raised his head to meet Archie's gaze. "I've surprised you."

"A little." Archie cocked his head. "Does Norah regret letting you 'win'? Do you ever discuss it?"

"No, to both questions. She couldn't love Piper more. But she never mentions how close the unspeakable came to happening. And no matter what, I never use that in an argument."

"That's some strong emotional intelligence. You described Norah as superintelligent. And yet you ended up with an unplanned pregnancy. Did you ever question how that happened?"

"I did. We weren't irresponsible. She was on the pill, but she had to do a course of antibiotics for an abscessed tooth, and that interfered with the birth control. She didn't trap me, if that's what you're implying."

"I had to ask. So, you hadn't been together long enough to discuss marriage, but you were together long enough to make a baby."

Sam nodded. "When Piper was born, I proposed again. This time, she said no because she didn't want to make a hormone-charged decision. Eventually, she told me she didn't believe we needed a piece of paper to legitimize our relationship."

Sam stood and walked over to the window. As he looked out at the street below, he said, "The biggest fight I ever had with my father was over the fact that I wasn't marrying Norah. Piper was about a month old—we'd finally gotten our feet under us, so we drove north to see my parents. She was their first grandchild, so I hoped..." He turned back to face Archie. "I hoped that she'd be the catalyst to mend fences."

He remembered Trent demanding that Sam join him outside after Sam told him he and Norah had no plans to marry. While his mother sat inside, cooing at her granddaughter, Sam had stood in the driveway, listening to his father belittle him. Joe had stood on the porch and watched the whole thing. No matter how many times Sam told Trent that Norah did not want to get married, it did nothing to thwart Trent's contempt.

After a moment, Sam plodded back to the couch.

"Where did you just go?" Archie asked.

Sam swallowed the lump in his throat and told Archie about the fight with his father. "That was the last time I went to their house until this past Thanksgiving." Sam guzzled half the bottle of water at his side.

Archie remained silent.

Sam took several deep breaths. "The night I ended it with Quinn, all those years ago. I had an engagement ring in my pocket." He had tucked that memory deeply away, only allowing it to surface when he saw her in Boston. "So, yeah, I believe in marriage."

Archie scratched some notes. "What do you think that means for your future?"

"It means there's no future for Norah and me, because now that I realize how much marriage means to me, I'm never going to be happy with less."

"That's a big step, Sam. How do you feel about it?"

"Strangely calm. When I came home to Joe dropping off the furniture, for a moment, I thought maybe Norah was coming back, and I wasn't sure if I wanted that. Now I know."

"'Calm' is a good word. You may still be sad about the loss of the relationship, but this is the start of a path forward. Let's change direction. Did you come up with an answer to my question from last time?"

"No." Sam looked toward the ceiling. "I guess if you can't go without a drink, if you're planning your day around having a drink, if you can't stop, that qualifies as problem drinking."

"Do any of those apply to you?"

"I made a conscious effort not to drink anything when Piper was with me these past two weeks."

Archie leaned back. "Were you successful at that?"

Sam nodded.

"What about the rest of the time?"

Sam sighed. "There were nights that I sat in front of the fireplace with a beer."

"Just one?"

Another sigh. "No." Sam clenched then unclenched his jaw. "I don't think that means I'm a problem drinker. Piper was with me for five days straight, and I didn't touch a drop of alcohol."

"You don't need to be defensive with me," Archie reminded him. "I'm not here to pass judgment."

"I know. It's myself I'm being defensive with. I have a constant internal dialogue going on about whether I should have a beer."

Archie drummed his fingers on the pad of paper on his lap. "Substance abuse is not my field of expertise, so you might want to take this with a grain of salt." He paused. "I don't believe you're an alcoholic. From everything you've told me, prior to

November, you did not drink heavily. You're seeking help to deal with your emotions. You're taking the right steps. But you see your drinking as a problem, so it is."

Sam nodded. "And you will not tell me what to do about it." He managed a grin.

"We can talk about options, but ultimately, it's your decision." Archie glanced at his watch then back at Sam.

Sam raised his eyebrows. "I haven't fallen apart."

"No, and you did some good work today." Archie grabbed a Post-it note from his desk, scribbled something on it, then handed it to Sam. "I sense that codependency could be an issue for you. This book is an excellent resource. We can talk about it next time."

Afterward, Sam sat in his car, drained. Reliving the argument with his father had been rough, even with the resulting clarification of his feelings about marriage. He really wanted a beer.

Sam shook his head. Piper would be with him that night, and he wouldn't give in to that craving.

Chapter Twenty-One

Family

SAM'S CAR HAD BARELY stopped in Jesse's driveway when Toni and Janey jumped out, followed by Piper. It had been a day off from school for all four kids, and Sam had taken the three girls skiing while Jesse took Diego to tryouts for an elite travel baseball team.

As they ran toward the house, Caitlin opened the door and raised a hand. "Antonia, Janey, you stop right there. Unload that gear from Sam's car! He's not your servant."

All three girls slowly made their way back to the car and retrieved the skis that Sam had removed from the roof rack.

Jesse and Diego pulled in beside Sam as he was removing ski poles from the trunk of his car. Jesse grabbed the poles to help.

Sam high-fived Diego. "How'd it go?"

"Good. Right, Dad?" Diego was almost dancing as he moved toward the house.

Sam could feel his excitement. He smiled and looked at Jesse.

Jesse shut the garage door and joined Sam. "It really did go well. He's so damn talented." Then he threw his arms around Sam. "You got the lead position. Congratulations! They made a good choice, the right choice."

"Thanks. I'm still having a hard time digesting it."

Caitlin met Jesse with a kiss. "It's going to be about half an hour before dinner is ready if you boys want to go down and have a drink. You must still be cold, Sam." She had congratulated him in the morning when he picked up the girls.

Jesse turned on the fireplace and poured two shots of bourbon. "I know you told me you are cutting back, but this'll warm you up."

"One's okay." Sam sank into the recliner. "It's good to be back here." Between work commitments and ducking out of work early on Mondays to see the therapist, Sam hadn't been to Jesse's house since Christmas. "Those dinners right after Norah left were a lifeline." He took a sip. "Ahhh, that is warm. The girls kept me out on the hill the entire day."

"We appreciate you taking them. We enjoyed that weekend we skied with you and Pip, but I needed to go with Diego today, and Cait wasn't up for being out there in the cold."

Sam smiled. "I loved it. Those two are going to be excellent skiers. You need to get used to the idea of being out in the cold, watching them race." He took another sip. "I'm glad you're in New Hampshire so Pip won't be competing against them. She's going to be good too." He leaned forward in the chair, reaching his hands toward the fireplace. "So, D did well in the tryout?"

"Too well." Jesse shook his head. "He's going to make the team, and it scares me. I know how the sport can take over your life. And I know how quickly that life can be destroyed." Jesse finished his bourbon. "But he wants it, and he's got the talent, so we'll support him as far as it takes him." He gestured toward Sam's empty glass. "A refill?"

"No, I'm serious about limiting myself to one."

"Archie was a good choice?"

"Yeah, and the ADHD meds are definitely making a differ-ence. Everything is easier."

"I'm glad to hear that. I should have recognized it. You owe a big thanks to Quinn."

Sam nodded. "I know."

"How are things with Norah? We didn't have time to talk on the ski trip with the kids around, and you've sent some cryptic texts."

Sam sighed. "Piper told the story at lunch that day." He elab-orated, adding, "Norah wasn't happy about it, maybe mostly because I hadn't told her about running into Quinn in Boston. We talked it out, but she was still annoyed."

"Did you tell her you slept together?" He paused, looking at Sam. "And more?"

"No, and thank God I didn't." Sam described trying to explain jealousy to Piper, then he leaned forward in the chair. "Norah still hasn't accepted that we won't be getting back together. She acted like nothing had happened when I saw her the next week, and she's been... very affectionate. I told you about Christmas Eve. She thinks I didn't want to do anything with her because I'd spent time with Quinn. There could be something to that, but honestly, the morning I walked out the door with her declaration about the move ringing in my ears, my desire turned to anger."

He stared into the fire. "While I'm getting a handle on the anger, the desire hasn't come back. Sex will not fix what's wrong between us."

"Which is?"

"I've let her dominate the relationship. Everything that happens is her decision. What I want hasn't mattered. She's made me feel like I'm part of the decision-making, but truly, I'm not. And it's not only with her. I was that way with Ginger and maybe even with Quinn." He rolled his eyes. "I'm the definition of pussy-whipped."

Jesse roared with laughter, and Sam joined him before saying, "But no more of that. I'm figuring out what I want."

Jesse nodded. "Do you talk to Quinn?"

"We text now and then. We're friends."

Jesse raised his eyebrows questioningly.

"I'm good with it." He laughed at the look on Jesse's face. "Really."

Jesse leaned back in his chair and smiled. "It's great to see how much happier you are."

"Thanks. Norah is taking Piper to Florida during February vacation, and I'll miss Pip, but I'm looking forward to the time alone. I never thought I'd get to this point. Norah asked me to go on the trip." He grimaced. "Another sign she's still hoping for a reconciliation. I'm wrestling with how to tell her that's not what I want."

After dinner, Sam lingered at the table, chatting with Jesse and Caitlin while Piper played in Janey's room. He stood and said, "I need to get Piper home. I hate these midweek days off. She'll never want to get out of bed in the morning." He yawned. "We need to figure out when we can do another ski weekend."

As Sam waited for Piper, Jesse stood behind Caitlin, and he rested his hands around her waist.

"Hey, Sam." Caitlin smiled and moved Jesse's hand to her belly. "I won't be skiing again this winter."

Sam saw their grins, and his eyes traveled to Jesse's hands. "Are you..."

"Yup," Jesse said cheerfully. "We're knocked up."

Sam wrapped his arms around them. "That's great! I'm excited for you." Then he pulled away. "You are happy about it, right? I'm surprised because I thought you were done after Janey. You told me one New England baby."

"We're happy, truly thrilled," Caitlin said. "Unexpected, but not unwelcome." She looked at Jesse. "We got careless."

"That we did." Jesse snickered. "We told the kids last night and asked them not to tell you so we could."

Caitlin laughed. "I can't believe both those girls kept a secret."

Piper came tearing down the stairs. "D-Daddy! Caitlin is going to have a b-baby!"

"I know!" Sam grinned at her. "They told me."

Piper fell asleep on the drive home, and as Sam lifted her out of the car, she woke up.

"D-Daddy, I'd like a b-baby brother or sister," she mumbled. "I wouldn't even care which."

Sam held her tight, and the same feeling he'd had months earlier washed over him. *I want more children.*

The End

Epilogue

SAM OPENED HIS LAPTOP, and while waiting for his email to load, he sent a text to Quinn.

> Sam: *I started taking ADHD meds a few weeks ago. I'm seeing a therapist, and he had me do a questionnaire. Turns out I'm an undisciplined mess who lacks focus. Lol. I think it's making a difference, so thanks for planting the seed.*

He had sent Quinn a few texts since they saw each other on the mountain, and she always responded but never initiated anything. It didn't surprise him—he suspected Caden occupied her free time. Sam was coming to accept that friendship was all there would ever be between him and Quinn.

Sam told her a little about his weekends on the mountain with Piper and wished her a good day at the end of their exchange. Later, he was working through his emails, deleting half and answering the rest, when a response to his Craigslist ad about his room for rent popped up.

I'm writing about the room you have to rent. I'm a 32-year-old single female and recently started a long-term sub job. My need is for a place through June, possibly longer. Can we meet soon to discuss details and see if our expectations are compatible? S Palmer.

A couple of traveling healthcare professionals had contacted Sam about the room, but they were only looking for a place for a month or two, and he was hoping for something longer. Some single men in their twenties had responded, but Norah's words had echoed in his mind, so he'd rejected them. He'd left the ad up but had little hope of finding the right tenant.

Does S Palmer realize I'm a guy? He'd signed the ad "Sam," which could be short for "Samantha." *Oh well, I'll see if she wants to meet. If she's not interested, I'll probably shelve the idea of renting the extra room.* The email included a telephone number, so he texted her.

> *Sam: Do you know Cara's Coffee Shop? I could meet you there tomorrow night at five.*

> *S: Yes, I know Cara's. Best donuts in the area. I'll see you then. I have dark-auburn hair, and I'll be wearing a hunter-green coat.*

Sam arrived at Cara's at exactly five and was glad to see only a few cars in the parking lot, nervous about the meeting, hoping he would recognize S Palmer. As soon as he walked in he saw Sophie sitting alone.

Oh my God. Dark-auburn hair, green coat. I'm such an idiot. His stomach lurched. *She's pretty.* He remembered her green eyes.

Sam approached the table with a smile on his face. "I'm having a sense of déjà vu. So, the *S* stands for Sophie?"

Sophie smiled. "I wasn't sure if 'Sam' was male or female. I didn't put two and two together."

Sam glanced toward Sophie's cup. "Let me grab a coffee. I'll be right back."

He returned with a mug and two donuts and slid the chocolate one across the table to Sophie as he sat down. "That's what you had when we were here before Christmas, right?"

She nodded and took a bite.

"I thought you were going to be done in mid-January," Sam said.

She swallowed. "That was the plan, but Ms. Thomas is now on bed rest for the rest of her pregnancy. I'm going to be here until the end of the school year. This might be awkward."

"Because you work at the school that Pip attends?"

Sophie nodded again.

"You don't work with her, do you? Will it go against some kind of school policy if you reside in a house where a student lives?" Sam washed down his bite of donut with a swallow of coffee. "This is a small town. It might be hard to avoid."

"No, I don't work with her, although she gets mentioned when we have department meetings." When Sam's face contorted, she shook her head, eyes wide. "Not in a bad way," she assured him. "All the children that we're working with are part of our discussions. And I know she's still stuttering."

"She is." Sam sighed. "You know, the thought of a new therapist working with Pip excited her mom and me. We're not unhappy with Mr. Donovan, but..."

A server refilled Sophie's cup, and he watched her take a sip.

"You're younger, more recently out of school," he said. "I think we both hoped you'd have some kind of magic wand."

"Regretfully, I don't, and Mr. Donovan is one of the best I've worked with." She paused. "Can you tell me a little about the house and why you're looking for a roommate?"

"It's a four-bedroom ranch. One bedroom is Pip's play-room, so it leaves me with one empty room, and I'm looking to bring in a little extra income." He showed her pictures of the house. "What's your story?"

"I'm only guaranteed a job through June, so it's too short a time to rent an apartment. I've been staying in a hotel, and that's too expensive." Sophie gazed out the window then back to him. "If this works out, maybe I could work with Piper informally."

"I don't want to ask you to do something for free when it's your livelihood," Sam said. "But I could forgo the damage deposit in exchange for your help."

"That's more than generous. Would I have designated space in the kitchen and fridge?"

"Of course."

"Can I work at the dining room table on weekday evenings? Sometimes I need space to spread out."

"I don't see that as any issue as long as you don't mind *Paw Patrol* running in the background." Sam grinned.

Sophie laughed. "That won't bother me. I block every-thing out when I'm working."

"Would you like to come see the place tomorrow?" Sam asked. "If you like it, you could move in then or on Sunday."

"I can come at tomorrow at ten," she said after a moment. Then she crumpled her napkin and stood. "Thanks for the donut."

After pizza at Norah's, Sam spent the night tidying up to prepare for Sophie's visit. He was doing better at housekeeping and knew his schoolwork was coming together more easily as well. He said another silent thank-you to Quinn for her perceptiveness.

Afterword

Did you enjoy this book? If you did, leaving a review on Amazon or Goodreads is a wonderful way to let the author know. Reviews are one of the most powerful tools in an author's arsenal.

Sneak Peak

Sophie looked out the window as she came out of her room. "Still snowing, huh. I was hoping to make it to the gym this afternoon."

Sam was reading on the couch. "It's not supposed to let up until late afternoon. The biggest storm of the winter."

A fire was roaring in the fireplace, and the living room was warm and welcoming. Sophie longed to sit down and enjoy it. "The fire is nice. It makes it cozy in here."

Sam smiled at her. "Join me."

She'd been renting the room for three weeks, and he'd offered her a glass of wine a couple of times, but she always declined, feeling like sharing a drink with her landlord might be inappropriate.

"We should talk about how thing are going. It's been almost a month... I hope you'll want to stay Pip loves having you here, and she's always my first concern."

Sophie blew out her breath, still too on edge to smile but relieved all the same. "This is working out well for me... Can we keep our arrangement open-ended? My contract only goes until the end of the school year."

"Of course."

Sophie nodded. "I'm going to get my book." She sat on the edge of the bed for a moment, happy and relieved she was going to be able to remain in Sam's house. It had been years since she'd felt this comfortable in a space. Still, doubts plagued her about sitting in the living room with him—and she could no longer deny it was because of a growing attraction she'd been unable to quell. Sam had given her no sign that he thought of her as anything other than a tenant, which she hoped meant she'd managed to hide her feelings.

When she came back with her book, Sam had fallen asleep on the couch, snoring softly. She curled up in a recliner and watched him for a few minutes before beginning to read. A sense of calm washed over her. After a while, she heard noises form Sam.

"Oh God, I fell asleep, didn't I?" Sam stretched as he sat up. "Looks like the snow has stopped, so now comes the shoveling."

"Do you want some help?"

"Sure." He looked at her, and his eyes narrowed. "Do you have a coat other than that green one?" That won't work very well for shoveling."

"I don't." Sophie tittered nervously.

Sam raised a finger before walking to his bedroom. When he returned, he tossed her a heavy sweatshirt. "This should work. It's not that cold out…"

Sophie pulled it over her head, drinking in the scent that she knew must be Sam's "Thanks."

Sam started her shoveling near the house. He was nearing the middle of the drive when he lobbed a snowball at her back.

She whirled around. "Hey, what was that?"

"You can't shovel without a few snowballs being thrown."

Sophie packed snow into a ball and threw it back at him. It him him square in the chest, and he staggered from the impact, then flashed a smile.

Oh God, that smile, *It does me in….*

As they walked inside, he said, "I have beef tips in the slow cooker. Do you want to join me for dinner?"

She paused then said, "That sounds delicious." She pulled the sweatshirt off and hung it to dry on a hook in the mudroom.

"It'll be about an hour before they're ready." Sam peeled off his shirt, and Sophie's heart skipped a beat. He turned to toss the shirt into a basket on top of the washer, giving her a view of his well-muscled abdomen, and her stomach twisted.

Does he know that he's torturing me."

Sam walked to his bedroom and came back buttoning a flannel shirt. "I'm going to have a beer. Would you like a glass of wine to warm up, or something else?" He put more wood on the fire as he was talking to her.

Sophie managed to squeak out. "Sure. I need to change into dry clothes."

She went to her bedroom and peeled of her jeans, replacing them with sweatpants. She took a couple of deep breaths, hesitating to return to the living room before she got herself under control. Because when Sam came back, wearing that partially buttoned flannel shirt, her lady parts had started throbbing and didn't seem remotely done yet.

Follow Sam and Sophie's story in Whispers of Change, coming on May 15, 2025.

Also by

Whispers of Goodbye
Whispers of Forgiveness
Whispers of Mistletoe
Whispers of Starlight

Acknowledgements

I hope you enjoyed Sam's story. I felt he had some growing to do before he could be successful in a relationship and now he's ready for more. This has been in my to be published bin for a long time and if I miss anyone who contributed to it, please forgive me.

Sally Walker and Sheryl Soffer were my critique partners throughout 2023 and had a great influence on Sam and his story. When I decided to add to his story, Sally was an important sounding board. I'll be forever grateful to both of them.

Thanks to Angie Gallion my content editor and Mary Morris, my line editor, both from Red Adept Editing. They make my words sing and have taught me so much about the craft of writing.

This, and all future books would still be sitting in that "to be published" bin if Emily Hensley of Small Fry Marketing had not come into my life. She gives me so much more than just marketing advice. Thank you.

My ARC team has been clamoring for this book and I'm grateful to them for their enthusiasm. It keeps me motivated.

My husband, Gordy, has taken over more and more of the day-to-day operation of our household, leaving me to work on all things related to writing. I only hope he knows how much I appreciate it.

And finally to my readers. I appreciate you spending some of your reading time with my books and hope you enjoy the stories as much as I do.

About the author

SUE IS AN AVID reader who ventured into the writing world during the first year of the Pandemic. Her stories showcase men and women working to become whole and happy. Family plays a prominent role as do the steamy encounters which come with falling in love.

Sue is a lifelong Vermonter who counts books, sunsets, and travel as vital to her being. Mountains, from the slopes of Vermont's Greens to the towering peaks of Colorado's Rockies feed her soul.

Her children are grown and flown and she's living her happily ever after with the boy she met in a college library fifty years ago.

Follow her on Facebook, Sue Mills – Author

Or on her website, suemillsauthor.com

Or on Instagram, suemillsauthor

And TikTok, Sue Mills, Author